# ONCE OR TWICE

A Novel

Corlan Arthur Carlson

*This book is dedicated to my history teachers from middle school, high school, university and graduate school levels. Not one of them could I have asked for more.*

# CONTENTS

# APRIL 1985

## PROLOGUE

The attic was the largest room in the house, big enough to store years of memories. It also had more than adequate lighting, due to her husbands improvements after they first bought the craftsman style bungalow in Portland. The two bedrooms below had managed to serve them and their twin daughters, but another bathroom had been added as one more of his projects. The place was cozy but just roomy enough, especially with the big back yard that the kids loved to play in. This was their first house, and now that he was gone she knew it would be her last, too. That was okay; she needed nothing more than what she had now in material terms, so why was she rooting through his old things in the attic? She knew the reason; she had wanted for a long time to know why he had died. People might think that there was always a specific reason for death, but she knew better. Sometimes it was a process shrouded in doubt, if not outright deceit.

After moving a couple of boxes aside, she spotted what she was looking for. It was an old fashioned briefcase, with hard shelled sides and a real clasp lock. It was battered and dusty, and the metals parts looked like they were beginning to rust. She had brought a screwdriver with her because she knew that her husband kept this particular item locked throughout their marriage. It would undoubtedly be necessary to break into it.

Before jamming the edge of the screwdriver into the crack between the halves of the briefcase though, she went ahead and tried to flip up the recessed metal snaps. "Oh, no. I don't believe it," she was muttering to herself as the case opened without forcing. She would not be able to explain her total surprise for this happening, except perhaps her two daughters. Their father had remained even more of a mystery to them than to her throughout his lifetime. The circumstances surrounding his death only guaranteed that fact would not change. Since the case opened so easily, she was asking herself why she had waited so long to search for answers.

A few sheets of loose paper fluttered out onto the attic floor. She noticed the dates on each as she gathered them up. Eight different dates on what looked like very old letters. She took a paper clip out of the pocket in her apron and clipped them together chronologically. Mina had been an organized, efficient wife and mother, and living alone had only increased her need to put things in order. She had been born sixty-six years ago to parents who were immigrants from northern Japan, who were very orderly, and who expected precisely the same from their children.

The rest of the briefcase contained three ring binders, with nothing loose in them. A quick appraisal revealed their contents concerned purchasing their home, investing their money, and birth certificates for their children. There were no certificates for either Mina or her husband James, and she didn't expect to find any. She turned back to the eight pages she had clipped together in order. She took in a sharp breath as she started to read the first page. Instead of continuing, she put them down, closed the briefcase, and retreated down the folding ladder from the attic. These letters required a close and thoughtful examination.

When she got downstairs she started boiling water for a large mug of tea. She also turned on the reading light above her easy chair and fluffed the pillow in it. Part of the reason she had been going though her husband's things was that her two daughters were coming to visit in a couple of hours. It might be a good time to talk to them about their father. She was going to study these missives one by one, very carefully. Perhaps her long period of waiting was going to have a worthwhile end.

# PART ONE

Tule Lake Segregation Center          10 January, 1944
Tulelake, California

My son,

I am sorry that my earlier letters (2) did not reach you. I did not know you had already moved from our farm clear over to Lakeview. I guess we were both relocated. I received nice letter from the newspaper editor in Lakeview. He explained the situation to me, including the knowledge that you had not heard from me. It also took me a good while to get permission to write and I had to use a english typewriter, no hand writing.

Now I understand that you are in a new school where maybe others don't know your parents. Mr. Carter also told me how you work in the yard of the church in Bly and help out in other ways around. He said you will still graduate in 1945 if you continue in the school and you will only be nineteen. Much better than if you are here. Your mother miss you but she is happy for your schooling.

Do not worry about us. We have food and a place to sleep. It is cold outside where I work but not so cold inside. I prefer you not to visit us here. Maybe soon we will go home. You work hard my son also, and do not worry. Help will come from above, you will see.

Your father, with much regard,

John Uschida

# LAKEVIEW, MAY 1945

## ONE

James carefully refolded the letter and put it back in his satchel. The crease marks in the paper were beginning to obscure some of the words but he knew them by heart anyway. He still wondered why they couldn't let his father sign the thing. The paranoia concerning immigrants from Japan, such as his parents, had no real logic to to it. They had worked so hard to make a decent living in the United States. When boarding the train to be relocated they had even then reminded James not to doubt the government here in their chosen land. Perhaps in the fifteen months since he had received this one and only letter from his father, his parents hopes and expectations might have changed.

He was sitting on the concrete steps of the house in Lakeview where he had boarded since his voluntary move eastward. He had finished his high school classes for the day, and dutifully mowed the lawn, all around the house, which he did on a weekly basis as part of his rent. It was the first day of May and the smell of newly mowed lawn mingled with the oil and gasoline odor from the old mower to create a sleepy, narcotic effect on his tired mind.

The owner of the home, Mr. Carter, had agreed with the school authorities in Klamath Falls that a new school would be in James' best interests. The written reasons involved the fact that he was a year behind his class in most subjects, as well as his "not fitting in" with students in the old school. That was code for the fact that he was a Japanese-American male who was tall for his age, only an inch below six feet, and therefore the subject of intense bullying by every short white kid who was trying to prove his manhood while their dad was away at war. The only reason behind his being held back in an earlier grade was his growing up in a home where English was not the first language. His age plus his smarts had enabled him to take the ugly treatment, but he was happy to transfer to his new school where most kids didn't know what to make of him. A few of the girls even thought the hints of tall, bronze stranger made him more attractive. To James, nothing at either school replaced the heart felt longing for his parents and two siblings that was eating at him now.

Before he could sink deeper into thoughts about his his separation from family he heard the click click of solid soled shoes striding purposefully down the sidewalk. Without lifting his head he knew Mr. Carter was coming home from the office. Almost every other man in this small town worked in the logging industry, and so they wore work-boots with small nails tapped into their soles. Those men sounded almost like tap dancers walking to the mill. Mr. Carter was editor of the daily newspaper, The Lakeview Gazette, and so he dressed the part; sport-jacket, white shirt and tie, not to mention the dress shoes.

"Hey there, James, the lawn looks mighty nice."

James smiled, "Hello, Mr. Carter, how are you?"

"I'm doing okay. And don't forget that you can call me Ben here at home." There were two copies of the latest newspaper folded under his left arm, while in his right hand was the neatly folded paper bag that held his lunch when he departed in the morning. He always kept one newspaper for his personal use while letting his wife and James share the other one. Not yet an elderly man, he was nonetheless fixed in many of his ways. He valued his place of influence in the small town, and maintaining that standing in society was as necessary as maintaining his lawn and flower beds. His life might have felt complete if he had a son, but the good lord had seen fit to bless him with two girls instead. Like many men, he had dreamt of being succeeded in his job by one of his children, but obviously that was not meant to be. One daughter was already married, while the youngest was at secretarial school clear down in San Francisco. She had only come back home once in two years and that was with her female roommate in tow, an older gal that Ben didn't warm up to during the visit.

"Scoot over there, James, and let an old guy sit down."

James quickly moved over. This was something new, Mr. Carter normally talked to him over dinner, not before then. He hadn't even gone inside and greeted his wife yet.

"I have something that I wanted to mention to you before you read it in the paper, son." While Ben Carter had been perfectly nice to him at all times, James had never heard him use the term son before, and he wasn't sure if he liked it. In Japanese, it wouldn't have sounded appropriate.

"Alright Mr. Carter, what it it?"

"As you will read in the paper tonight, Adolf Hitler committed suicide yesterday while he was hiding in an underground bunker in Berlin. A new government in Germany is now negotiating terms of surrender to the Allied Forces. The war in Europe will officially end in a few days. They already have a name for it. It's going to be called V-E day, short for victory in Europe, and people can't wait to start celebrating."

"Wow! That's great news, for sure."

"Yes, it absolutely is. A lot of our boys will be coming home, some of them pretty soon, I wager. But here's the thing, James. The war in the Pacific is still far from over. Some troops might even be transferred out there from Europe without stopping in the States, I don't know. But I do think it's possible that the war with Japan may get even more intense."

"What do you mean?"

"I'm talking about a possible invasion of Japan by American troops, maybe even use of one of the new megabombs that we are supposed to have under development, something like that. We really don't know much right now. But one thing I do believe is that intensifying the conflict over there could have ramifications here at home."

James looked straight at Mr. Carter, "I think I understand what you are saying. In other words there could be more anti-Japanese feelings aroused."

"That's right. In a sense your folks might be better off than you over the coming months because they are in the camp at Tule Lake. They could be more protected than a young man like you. Of course you have kept your head down, and not gotten into any kind of trouble the whole time you have been here. After school you are working hard here and at the missionary church in Bly. To be completely frank, you are also lucky that many of the local folks think you look like a member of one of the Indian tribes around here. That's helped, believe me. Anyway, just continue to mind your P's and Q's, and I think we'll be okay."

Ben Carter stood up and James understood that the conversation was over. He stood too, and held the door while Mr. Carter strolled into the house. Sitting back down, the concrete steps felt not one bit harder than the questions he was now facing. Would his careful planning be disrupted? He was so close to graduation. Afterwards, he had already decided to leave the west coast for a midwest college, if his dreams panned out. He felt that his life was about to change, but in what direction? Like his parents he desperately wanted to work hard and succeed, but in a place where his every move wasn't being watched.

*****

Dinner was served in the Carter household at 6:30 every evening. They ate in the dining room for this meal and on nice dinnerware using cloth napkins. The timeframe allowed Mr. Carter to return home from work, take off his jacket and tie, fix himself a nice martini, and read over the same newspaper which he had undoubtedly read more than once while it was being produced. At home however, he had the time to circle remaining errors of any kind and jot down comments that some unfortunate staffer would hear during the morning meetings at the office or the print shop.

James enjoyed Alice Carter's cooking. Somehow the fact

was that rationed items were more available to one with Mr. Carter's standing in the community. That meant even pot roast with potatoes and carrots a couple of times each week. Tonight Alice had a nice cardigan on and her hair pinned up, which usually signaled a better plate of food to James. Still, he did miss the fresh vegetables that his mother would harvest from their huge garden, a garden so big that city dwellers like the Carters might consider it a small farm.

He wondered what the home place looked like now that his parents had been relocated. He simply didn't have the time to get back there, with all of his odd jobs to do, plus graduating on schedule. Their acreage was located southeast of Klamath Falls, close to the California border, and there were no straight roads going over the mountains to get there. That was not to mention that his beat-up Ford Model-T had been on it's last legs for several years before he bought it from the scrap yard.

The big news about the war had both Alice and Ben in a talkative mood at dinnertime. Alice brought up the subject of Japan. "What do you think this news means to the Japanese high command, Ben?"

"I don't really know the answer to that, of course, just like our commanders probably don't know. I have heard some interesting rumors recently from Steve, you know, the newspaper editor over in Burns."

"What did he have to say?"

"Well, first of all, he said that he had been told not to pass on one particular rumor by his local military liaison."

"Oh, I see. If the War Department says not to talk about it, then that must mean there's some truth to it."

"Exactly. What I've been told is that a rancher and his son

appear to have found some kind of balloon, with an incendiary device of some sort attached to its guide lines. There were Japanese scratchings, either words or numbers, I don't know what to make of their symbols, on the device. But there was no doubt who made it. Anyway, it hadn't exploded or burned anything either."

"But how would something like that get to central Oregon from the Far East?" James rarely interjected himself into dinnertime conversations, but he was highly intrigued by what Mr. Carter was saying.

"They must be launching them from ships in the eastern Pacific, I guess," replied Ben. "As you know we were warned earlier in the war about possible Japanese marine landings on the Oregon coast. That's why the Lincoln County militia was formed, to hold invaders at bay until the military could get a handle on things."

"Don't we have big balloons of our own stationed up at Tillamook?" was James' next question.

"Those are dirigibles, lad. They are huge air vehicles that are manned and flown on patrol up and down our coastline and out to sea. But yes, I see what you are getting at. Why didn't our big war balloons spot the little Japanese war ballon, if that's what it was?"

"Ahem," Alice cleared her throat. "Maybe I shouldn't say this, but if we keep it in this room, I think it's okay."

"Say what, dear?" Ben was staring at her.

"Why couldn't a smaller balloon like the one the ranchers found have been launched from somewhere inland? Then the blimps would not have spotted it. Perhaps there are Japanese sympathizers operating here in Oregon. Or maybe it was sent up into the air by detainees at the relocation center down at Tule Lake."

James was silent now, but his mind was reeling. He had

never heard Alice talk about this subject. Was she actually accusing people like his parents, who were confined at Tule Lake, of working for the enemy? Or could she possibly be indirectly pointing her finger at someone like himself?

James was among a very few "Nisei" exceptions to relocation. Nisei meaning second generation Japanese-Americans with citizenship based upon birth in the United States. That status by itself was no exemption from being interned, of course. Asian ethnicity was the only basis for internment, as some Koreans, traditional enemies of the Japanese, had discovered to their amazement. But James had done two things. During the first couple of weeks of a flurry of military orders he had relocated out of the government designated section one on the west coast by voluntarily moving from the Klamath Falls area to Lakeview. Once there he had wrangled college scholarship assistance using a program for immigrants facilitated by the Quakers. The offer was good after he finished his senior year at Lakeview High, where he was under the Carter's sponsorship. There were religiously based colleges in several midwestern states still accepting Japanese-American applicants.

"You're right about one thing, my darling. This subject should not be talked about outside of our home." Mr. Carter was still staring at Alice, perhaps with a slight bit of alarm in his eyes, or at least that's what James thought. "There is probably a rational explanation for whatever those Bend guys found, so we shouldn't do or say anything to rile folks up unnecessarily."

After dinner James retreated to his room upstairs to study for his geometry test in the morning. In the past he had often sat in the living room studying, but tonight he wasn't sure he would feel comfortable there.

****

The Christian Evangelical church in Bly was closed and locked tight on Thursday afternoon. The weather felt abnormally dry and warm for May on the north pacific coast, but Bly was just over the crest of the coastal mountains and so enjoyed more sunshine in the spring than any Oregonian had a right to. Rhododendrons and other bright bushes around the sides of the small white clapboard church were flowering, some of their blooms almost matching the mahogany tint in James thick, dark hair as he raked underneath them. Honey bees were making all kinds of noise as they traversed from blossom to blossom, a sound that reminded James of the vegetable garden at home. He had finished mowing and was now cleaning out the flower beds before he checked the trash cans and swept the sidewalks.

He heard the sound of gravel crunching as a small sedan pulled into the parking area and then the scrunch of an emergency brake being yanked. He stepped out of the bed to see who was there and was unsurprised to observe Pastor Charlie getting out of his vehicle. The minister of the church was an engaging young man who always had a smile and a warm greeting for James. He had gotten married a short time back and that fact, coupled with his deep belief in the scriptures, tended to make him a very upbeat guy.

It looked to James like there was someone else in the car, probably his wife, but they weren't budging out of their seat and he didn't want to stare. He did wave hello to the minister, however, and was surprised to see him both wave back and then head his way. He put down his tools and gloves so he could shake Charlie's hand.

"Hello, Mr. Turnbull," he said quietly.

"Howdy, James, how are you?" was the earnest reply.

"Oh, I don't know, just normal I guess," shrugged James, kind of curious why he was getting the full greeting that most actual parishioners got, when he was just a gardener. Charlie had asked him about his faith, of course, prior to hiring him. James had said that he was a Christian. When the pastor had asked what kind of Christian, James had replied 'your garden variety kind of Christian'. Since he was applying for a gardening position he thought that was a pretty funny reply, but at the time Charlie just sort of looked at him curiously.

"Well, I wanted to let you know something. Eleanor and I are taking some of the Sunday School kids on a picnic the day after tomorrow. I thought maybe you would want to come along. We're driving up towards Gearhart Mountain in the national forest. If you were here working Saturday morning, then you could leave afterwards with us. You might like to meet some of the Sunday School children.

James replied politely, "I'm sorry, pastor, but that won't work for me. I have stuff to do for other people that morning in Lakewood, and it's too much of a drive for me to do in a short time." Underneath a calm exterior, he was thinking that he didn't have the time to get involved with extra church activities in Bly, and that he was obviously too mature for the Sunday School kids.

"Oh, well okay then. I'm going to grab some things out of my office and take off, my wife's waiting. Nice job on the flower beds, by the way. Enjoy your day of rest on Sunday."

TWO

Rather than resting on Sunday, James was sweating mightily as he cranked and cranked the engine of his model T. It was a warm afternoon, which usually meant that the dang engine would turn and start over more quickly, but not today when he really needed it to. After listening to an agonizingly slow sermon at the Carter's Lakeview church, and doing his homework faster than a tornado, he was on his way back to Bly. He needed to get there as quick as possible and help out anyway that he could.

The whole town had been completely stunned by the horrendous news that spread like a wildfire Saturday evening. Pastor Charlie, his wife, and five young Sunday schoolers had been hit by some kind of an explosion while they were out picnicking yesterday afternoon. Four of the children were dead, as well as the ministers wife, who was with child. There were rumors that a fifth child had died at the hospital here in Lakeview. Meanwhile Charlie had serious burns from trying to rescue those under his charge, but word was that he was going to be okay, at least physically. Mentally and emotionally was another matter, as those in the community who had dealt with wounded veterans of the current war knew full well.

Mr. Carter had been fulminating since the news came down the mountain. He was of the opinion that the bomb had to be similar to the one found in the Bend area. He had pleaded with the government censors to let his paper cover the finding of another explosive device in central Oregon but they had steadfastly refused. No war information at all could be released without their blessing and they claimed that this incident might be war related, while at the same time telling him not to worry about it. Talking out of both sides of one's mouth simultaneously must have been a hiring requirement for the War Department.

Even when he took a short break from the cranking James was shaking nervously. Everything had seemed so normal when he conversed with Charlie the day before yesterday. Now he felt like his world was coming apart. The message that he had received from Alice at dinner Tuesday night was also reverberating inside him. He instinctively knew there were people in both Bly and Lakeview who would try to place blame on Japanese sympathizers for this event. He could hear them now, claiming that internees at Tule Lake might have snuck out of the camp at night to plant bombs. Maybe even worse, as Mr. Carter suggested, it might have been the kind of bomb sent via balloon from an off-shore Japanese ship or perhaps launched from a submarine that had surfaced. Was this quiet rural area really under attack from the last enemy left standing in this damned interminable war? Nothing made sense yet, which made it much worse than if he knew what the actual situation was. He was confused and scared; but he wasn't going to let that stop him from being helpful to people, like Pastor Charlie, who had been nothing but helpful to him. As the kids he faced down at his old high school knew, James would never start a fight, but he would never run, either.

The engine roared to life after his last crank and he dropped his head in exhaustion and gratitude. He wanted to get up there in the mountains while it was still light, see what he could do, and then return before the official curfew that applied to Japanese-Americans started at ten p.m. Since he was the only one in Lakeview affected by the silly proclamation, it had never been an issue before, but he was certain this horrific event in Bly meant things were going to be very different from now on.

His emotions quieted as he got moving on the road. The drive up through the hills towards Bly was as scenic today as it had ever been. The air was fragrant with wild grasses and scattered sagebrush in the lower elevations. When the tall, sturdy Ponderosa pine trees came into view they were resplendent with the late-day sun seeming to explore every crimson crevice in their dark brown bark. Sap was flowing in the spring down the newer Ponderosas and the hint of vanilla in it replaced the sage. There was little to no traffic between Lakeview and Klamath Falls on a Sunday afternoon but that didn't matter to James in his model T. He wasn't able to pass any vehicle on the road except farm machinery in his jalopy, a vehicle that fell somewhere on the spectrum between antique and just plain ancient.

\*\*\*\*\*

There were a few cars parked on the nearby streets, but little evidence that anyone was inside the church in Bly. Perhaps the townspeople had retreated to their homes in order to grieve. James was going to try to find Charlie and attempt to express his condolences. He was also going to ask if there was anything special Charlie wanted him to do for the upcoming services, either to the church, it's yard, or for the Pastor personally. He parked in the small lot next to the church and got out of his car quietly.

As he did so several people began to emerge from the front door of the building. Since James didn't attend services here, most of them were unrecognizable to him, although one or two seemed vaguely familiar. As he walked to the entrance he nodded and smiled at each one as they passed but received only looks ranging from indifference to perhaps a little suspicious. When he reached the door, one last parishioner was backing though it while carrying a cooking dish in her arms. James held the door open for the woman and then turned towards her with a final smile.

He was completely unprepared for what hit him. Right in the face. She had spit at him before turning to walk away. He stood there holding the door open with saliva dripping off the side of his jaw, and his legs feeling bolted to the ground. He simply could not comprehend what had just happened. No one else appeared to have noticed, and the woman was scurrying down the sidewalk towards her car.

James stepped inside the church, took one more stride, and sank to one knee in the entrance alcove. He drew one of the gardening rags out of his back pocket and wiped his face clear. A sound was sticking in his throat, halfway between a sob and a cry of outrage. Only a strange moan was emerging however, as Pastor Turnbull entered the alcove from the sanctuary on the other side. James tried to swallow and straighten his back when he saw the man. For his part, Charlie looked confused at seeing the gardener on an off day and on his knees prior to even entering the sanctuary.

"James! What is it?" Charlie was looking into his eyes as he lowered himself to one knee to talk on his level. The pastor was flat out the nicest guy James had ever met, while at the same time not being of the patronizing sort. "I'm sorry, James. Perhaps I should have called to let you know what happened. And to tell you that I'm doing okay now."

James was noticing the bandages on the minister's hands and forearms, as well as large yellow smudges above them. There were what appeared to be small bruises on his face and the sent of sulphur was quite noticeable. Reciprocating Charlie's direct eye contact, he noticed the minister's damp eyes were filled with sadness. The man had obviously been crying earlier.

"Oh, it's nothing, Pastor. I just wanted to see if I could help out up here in any way."

Charlie sank to his other knee and put an arm around James' back. "Thank you. There are so many people who have come forward to help me in the last twenty-four hours. There is such love in this community."

James knew he simply couldn't share with this grieving man that there were also people filled with hatred instead of love in his community. Now was absolutely not the time. The minister was shaking slowly, sort of a whole body vibration emanating from emotions that James could hardly fathom. What did it feel like to suddenly lose both the woman you just married and your unborn child? James immediately felt that he was here for one purpose, to comfort Charlie, and consideration of his own recent treatment would be rude and out of place.

He reached out with his left hand and held the pastor's shoulder. The two of them remained stationary on their knees on the floor and said nothing to each other for what seemed like a long time.

Then the minister slowly rose to his feet. "You don't need to do anything more, James, thanks. I've been asked to dinner by one of the church families. I need to stop at the parsonage and clean myself up some, and put on a tie. But I can't thank you enough for coming, James. Somehow, I just knew that you would."

James very slowly replied, "I wish with every bone in my body that I had accepted your invitation to the picnic. I would have been there to help you yesterday."

"But James, you might have been one of the ones who died, too. Listen to me now, after any event that occurs, we can't alter what happened. That's the past. But what we can do is try to take the right path in the future." Charlie paused for a  moment and then continued, "I remember you saying one time that you were a garden variety Christian, James. Well, in my opinion that's all that you need to be. The savior himself spent some time in gardens, such as Gethsemane, didn't he? I'll see you next week, when you come back to work. Blessings on you."

After the pastor quietly exited the front doors of the church James waited a moment and then peeked though them to see if anyone else was still outside. He quickly walked back to his model T and started cranking. There was no quiet way to crank and he glanced carefully around the car to see if anyone was listening, but again it seemed the townspeople had retreated.

*****

As he motored down through the hills in the twilight thoughts were flowing out of James mind faster than the trees were going by. There were so many details of the bombing that he desperately wanted to know. Was the device attached to a balloon like up in the Bend  area? Where did it come from? Unfortunately, he knew the wartime censors might already be at work damping down speculation, rumor, and of course, facts. He also knew that he couldn't ask Charlie for details any time soon. As forgiving as he knew the man to be, his double loss would have to leave him with guilt, as well as remorse. James would have to be extra careful who else he asked, too. This event would change so many lives. Charlie was injured more than he let on, and his wife, a beloved member of the community was dead. There were also five children from Bly dead. There was the distraught parents of the young children, children killed by what they must have thought was a plaything. Then there was all their fellow members of the Bly church. Although it appeared that their pastor intended to stay, what would be their  feelings when looking at his anguished face?

Last, and certainly least, people like himself. Would his life ever be the same? Would he ever be able to walk the streets in Bly or Lakeview or Klamath Falls without fear of insults or slurs against his perceived ethnicity? Was the woman who despised him and spat upon him a sister or mother of one of the victims? After reflecting on events, he couldn't help it if concerns about himself, his father and mother, and his siblings began to gradually dominate the other thoughts in his mind. What would the future bring to him and his family? If a peace like the one in Europe ever came to the Pacific theater, would that really change anything?

It was after dark and dangerously close to the ten o'clock curfew when he got back to the Carters. All of the lights were out, hopefully meaning that they thought he was upstairs in his room when they went to bed. As he walked up the front stairs with his key in his hand he felt that for the first time in his life he was grateful for the darkness.

# PART TWO

15 June, 1947          *Tillamook Naval Air Station*

*Tillamook Beach, OR*

Dear James,

    I have received and studied your letter. It is an usual inquiry for a base commander to deal with. Eighteen months ago I would have replied that everything you are asking about is classified. But as you probably know, everything is changing rapidly at this time. That includes the disestablishment of many wartime facilities and all local military liaison officers. This entire base is scheduled to be closed next year. Even our nationwide dirigible defense program seems destined for the dustbin of history. Jet engines, of course, are the future.

    The bottom line is that several of your questions about the Japanese balloons launched in the closing days of the War in the Pacific can now be answered, at least in part. Rather than going into a detailed technical assessment, I think your idea of visiting our facility this summer is what you should do. I can have my adjutant schedule your visit and then have one of my officers answer those questions that he deems appropriate. Certainly your desire to help locate any other balloons that may have landed inside the state is a noble pursuit. Obviously, coordination with local policing jurisdictions must be done prior to collecting and attempting to dispose of any found explosive devices.

    I look forward to meeting you, young man.

*Lt. Commander Chase Cunningham*

*Acting Commander, Naval Air Station*

# TILLAMOOK, JUNE 1947

## ONE

His new car was a Ford model A, much better than the old model T, but still far from meeting any definition of the term 'new'. James had purchased it from the same scrapyard that had inflicted the model T on him, but he had enough funds now to get the parts necessary for it to function properly. Plus, he could install them himself. So far, on his trip up the Oregon coast to Tillamook, it was running well. He had even passed a slower car on the coastal highway, which was an entirely new maneuver for him.

The curvy highway did not lend itself to speed, of course. The views to his right of the coastal mountain range, covered with evergreens, were impressive, but nothing like the ocean view on the other side. It was a scene he had never before experienced. When the road was up high and close enough to the edge to look at the waves crashing against huge rock formations, he more than once was mesmerized to the extent he almost drove off the road, nearly joining the commotion below. Raucous birds were soaring upwards from the water and flashing in front of his windshield. While fixated on the view to his left, at first he didn't notice a bull Elk with a full rack strolling out from the woods on the right side of the road. The animal swung it's head, he swerved, and his right side mirror cleared the horns with about an inch to spare. He began thinking the drive was more thrilling than any one he had experienced at the county fair.

James was working part time as an accountant for an insurance company in Klamath Falls, thus the extra money for car parts. He was also helping his parents resurrect what was left of their small farm when they returned from the Tule Lake internment center. College had only lasted two years for him; there was simply too much going on with the war ending, his family reuniting, and his single minded quest to discover more balloons before other injuries occurred.

In order to gain access to Tillamook Naval Air Station he had a the letter from Lt. Commander Cunningham, the acting base commander. While the war had been over for almost two years he knew that calls would have to be made before the grunts at the gate would allow someone who looked like him access to the base. As it turned out, getting through included a full search of his vehicle and himself, as well as some sharp questioning. Nevertheless, as he drove across the field towards the huge dirigible hangers, his spirits were high. He had made a promise to himself to take some sort of action to help heal the terrible wounds from May 5th, 1945 in Bly, and he thought perhaps things were starting to fall in place.

Now that he was drawing closer, the size of the hangars was amazing to him. He hadn't seen any buildings half that tall at the Klamath Falls airbase. The fact that these behemoths were built of wood was also a wonder. It made them a very complex and expensive project, but during the war winning had become all that mattered. He would be meeting Cunningham at the first one; that was the only guidance he had been given after he cleared the gate. He didn't know if that meant the commanders office was there or if a short tour of the hangars was in the works first. He parked in the big lot, which was mostly empty, and tossed the temporary parking permit on the dash board. With a notebook and a pen he set off to the meeting. The sunshine and pleasant weather outside didn't prepare him for the climate he encountered inside, however.

The moment he walked through the big doors, the temperature and light diminished sharply. It was like entering a cavern that hadn't seen the sun since the beginning of time. He felt moisture on his bare arms and looked upward to see what was going on. He swore it looked like mist at the very top of the giant structure. Peering around, it took a while for his eyes to adjust to the gloominess.

Striding towards him was a tall man in an immaculate white uniform and an officers hat brimmed with gold braid. The imposing figure stopped immediately in from of him and stuck out his hand, "I'm Lt. Commander Cunningham. You are James Uschida, I take it."

"Yes, sir." James involuntarily reacted with a military precision that he had never possessed.

"No, no, don't call me sir. I get enough of that from everybody else on this base. I don't need it from civilians. How about I call you James and you call me Chase."

"That's fine, Mr. Cunningham."

The officer started chuckling, "Well, whatever works. I thought that we would take a walk around one of our dirigibles while we talk a little about the Japanese war balloons that you referenced in your letter. I don't have permission to share everything we know with you, but I think that I can help some with your ideas about containing the danger. There's a desk where you can jot down notes when we're finished, but I'm afraid that I do need to look over the notes before you leave."

"That's fine, Mr. Cunningham, I want to comply with all the rules around here."

The Commander gave a smile that seemed genuine to James, and then started to briskly walk towards the airship while rattling off information at a rapid clip. The briefing had begun in earnest.

*****

By late afternoon James had finished his visit and driven from the base to a camping area by Cape Lookout, a lighthouse on the coast a few miles west of Naval Station Tillamook. He had erected his small tent, chopped some wood for an evening fire, and then strolled to the top of the big sand dune between him and the shore. He was staring out to sea, almost hypnotized by the endless waves. Their rhythmic sound, as regular as a metronome, contributed to his somber, reflective mood.

He was thinking about what Cunningham had told him concerning the future of the dirigibles. The entire program was in the process of being shut down, and that would make a military presence on the Oregon coast superfluous. Or, to use the militaries vernacular, everything was subject to being surplussed. The dream that existed in James mind, namely that American flying balloons could be used to help locate any remaining Japanese war balloons that had crashed, was not going to be on anyone's agenda. His days as a squadron leader over, Cunningham had been very straightforward with him concerning the future of the base. He had also been humble enough to point out that someone of higher rank than himself would have been in charge if the place was not already deemed obsolete.

The only suggestion that Cunningham had for James was to coordinate with local forestry officials and try to get a few of the fire fighters who were not in action to assist James and others in ground searches over potential landing areas. Since one of the aims of the war balloon program had been to initiate forest fires, it made sense to the commander that officials in the federal Department of Agriculture, which ran the forest service, would be more interested than the War Department mucky-mucks. Unfortunately, James had already talked to local forestry people in the office at Lakeview and they had other issues higher on their to do list.

When James asked the Lt. Commander what was going to happen to him after the base closed, he couldn't have been more surprised at the answer. Cunningham was leaving the military and he offered more than one reason. The lack of promotions in a peacetime military. An absence of purpose now that the fascist powers had been defeated. Most surprising; a desire to pursue an artistic career. Art had been his minor in college and Chase Cunningham wanted to be a painter.

Like most able bodied young American males, he had joined the armed forces after Pearl Harbor. Enrollment in the ROTC program at the University of Idaho plus a few basic flying lessons were enough to convince somebody somewhere that he might make officer material. He took so much time being trained to fly dirigibles however, that he had been one of the lucky few servicemen whose assignments were all in the United States. He felt like patrolling the coast was important but still, duty only in the lower 48 states wasn't the same as serving in a combat theater.

When they walked outside the hangar, James pumped his hand as they parted and told him he valued his service. The Lt. Commander had replied by motioning west toward the Pacific ocean and saying, "There are plenty of troops now at home who engaged in hand to hand combat with the enemy on some god forsaken island out there, James. They deserve all the credit in the world. I just want to get on with my life, never forgetting those guys, but not dwelling on all the horrific past events, either."

The sun was starting to set by the time James finished ruminating about his visit. He stared out into the all encompassing body of water  trying to see the horizon line, the absolute last place where the emptiness of the water blended into the lightness of the sky. Yes, there were hundreds of islands out there beyond the horizon, and the birthplace of his parents, Japan, was one of them. Tens of thousands of people had died on that island, too, and he just couldn't make sense of it. Why weren't all human beings able to get along as easily as Lt. Commander Cunningham and he had gotten along? When did people start to hate others simply because they didn't look exactly like themselves?

He had enough questions to fill the ocean he was staring at, but he possessed damn few answers. Finally, he shook himself out of his trance, swiveled around on the dune, and ambled down to his little tent. Perhaps tomorrow would bring him every answer he needed. On the other hand one wave large enough to top the dune he just walked down would end his need for them.

## TWO

The drive was long and hot. Even leaving the coast at the break of dawn, James had only made it to Bend before his car and his willpower both seemed at a stopping point. He had camped again the previous night since motel money was something he didn't have. Fortunately he chose a spot next to the Deschutes River and that gave him fresh water to spot bathe in. As cold as it was, it was better than the salt water he had used when visiting Tillamook. He had another two days off before he needed to be back to work, and so he was taking a scenic route today through parts of the state that he had never seen. He was relying on the map always stashed in his car and he intended to stop whenever he could to make sure he was on the right road. Most of south central Oregon was so lightly populated that neither food nor gasoline were readily available. Making it from one oasis of civilization to the next without incident was a good idea in this outback.

The town of Plush was next on his itinerary, and he couldn't help wondering how a place in the middle of nowhere received such a weird name. About thirty miles north of town, he stopped at a wide spot in the two lane road and slowly pulled onto the sandy shoulder. He hadn't seen anyone going either direction for the last half an hour. He grabbed his pair of binoculars, exited his car, and then leaned against it while stretching every muscle; arms, legs, and shoulders, that had stretch left.

The sound of absolute emptiness, a complete and total silence, was causing his ears to recalibrate. The din of the car engine was now gone. The only wind he had been hearing was caused by the movement of the car. There were no trees within fifty miles in any direction, he heard no bird sounds, nor any rustle in the underbrush. Simply an enveloping, dead stillness. He hadn't experienced solitude like this before and for a brief moment he entertained the thought of being alone on earth.

Quickly discarding that unpleasant idea, he pivoted to the east where there was a dark indigo ridge that formed a looming presence in the impossibly blue sky. Checking his map, he found that Hart Mountain was its name. Turning westward he could see another ridge farther off, lining the horizon. This one had a much sharper edge, appearing like a cliff face from this distance. From his Oregon state history class in high school he knew that he was looking at the Abert Rim, which marked the western border of the Great Basin, a mammoth interior desert that had been a tremendous travail to wagon trains heading for the coast of California or Oregon. The smell of surrounding small bushes; sage, rabbitbrush, and mahogany, lent an intoxicating ambience to the still air. As he stood there so silently he could hear his own breathing he knew, for some inexplicable reason, that this trip would turn out to be a very important part of his destiny. James sensed he was at a turning point, but like his earlier meditation on the sand dune he was lacking an answer as to why.

The ramshackle general store in Plush had plenty of food,

and even an old ice block freezer with ice cream in it for sale. More important was the single gas pump in front of the store that allowed him to fill up the tank. A pleasant middle aged woman behind the till politely asked what he was doing in the area.

"I'm driving back to Klamath Falls after a visit to the coast."

"Well, dearie, you must have taken a wrong turn.," she was smiling as she talked.

"No, I'm just taking the scenic route. I've never been in this neck of the woods. Uh, well, I guess there aren't that many woods around here."

She smiled, "Do you have a place to stay in Lakeview tonight? That's the nearest town with a hotel."

"Oh, I'm just roughing it. I'm young enough not to need a soft bed every night".

"If that's the case, I've got an idea for you."

"Sure, I'd like to hear it, ma'am."

"If you take the Hart Mountain Road out of town it will wind up to the top of the ridge, which is what Hart Mountain really is, just one long ridge system."

"What's up there?"

"Nothing. That's what makes it such a nice camping spot. There are views of the entire valley, of course. And lots and lots of antelope, Oregon Pronghorn antelope. They are magnificent creatures. And there's a natural hot springs to bathe in."

"Oh, really?" The idea of a hot bath was suddenly appealing to James.

"Yes sir. It's a nice size and pretty deep. Paiute hot springs they call it. Named after the natives up there in the desert. Head south on a spur off the main road after you go over the ridge top. That road is kind of shaky, more like two trails than a road, but you'll get there. You know, being young and tough and all."

James thanked her and strolled back outside. Was she possibly putting him on, he wondered? Maybe playing a practical joke on a naive, Japanese looking outsider? Still feeling that there must be a reason for his venture into the outback, he decided to drive up to the top of Hart Mountain anyway. What did he have to lose?

*****

It wasn't a joke. The road up the mountain, though unpaved of course, was as wide and smooth as a dirt road could be. The scenery, once he reached the top, matched in a certain way his oceanside outlook. This time he was looking at a veritable sea of sagebrush, a desert that seemed to stretch forever northward. The green color with a tinge of blue that blanketed the land below was akin to the blue-green waters of the Pacific. The air was still warm up high and it hadn't lost its wonderful smell. The road south to the hot spring was unmarked and the further he bounced and jolted through the high desert the more he wondered whether he had remembered the directions correctly. After passing a rusted old pickup to the side of the single track he felt that he must be nearing the hot springs. Finally he saw a small, weather beaten wood sign that had Paiute Springs scrawled on it. There were no other cars around, and no one seemed to be camping here, although some of the sagebrush was tall enough to hide a small tent.

The first thing James did was put up his two man pup tent tent. He knew from experience not to walk around or do other things before that because the weather could change rapidly and night would fall while you're not really noticing. After he had tossed his sleeping bag and pillow inside the tent, he gathered some of the dried mahogany branches lying on the ground for a fire. At last he grabbed a towel and a bar of soap from his duffle bag. His swim suit was still damp from a brief dip in the river last evening, but when one was alone in the middle of nowhere, there was no need for any type of swimwear.

There were small sulphur clouds emanating from a rift in the ground about thirty yards from his car signaling the hot springs location. The smell wasn't great but it was being wafted away from the pool towards the east by a slight breeze. He walked softly, checking for snakes as he approached the springs. It was a bigger pool than he thought when he arrived, due to it's being so cleverly hidden by the surrounding rocks and vegetation. The water was gently bubbling to the top in one or two places, while motionless for the most part. One issue he took note of was that the sage and other plants overhung the water, with the surface of the pond being two to three feet below the ground level. This would make getting in and out more challenging. After stripping his clothes off and tossing them on a rock, he sort of half slid down the overhanging branches and half jumped into the hot spring. He went completely under the surface at first, but quickly paddled back to the top, reaching over to grab a thick plant root and stabilizing himself with one foot against the rocky side.

The water was wonderful. It was very warm, but not too hot, and amazingly relaxing. He felt his arm muscles, tired from all the driving begin to instantly unwind themselves. He lowered himself to chin level and his shoulders and his backbone all the way up to his neck were massaged by the gentle current flowing upward from the deep source of the hot springs. He was wondering whether he might be falling asleep when he heard a soft voice say to him, "You sure made a big splash getting in here, bucko."

"What?" said James, swinging his head wildly around him trying to locate the source of the sound.

"Over here," the voice insistently said, "over here."

Gradually he made out a shape under one of the overhanging bushes on the other side of the pool. It was a female face, with long black hair floating on the water next to it. He peered intently and then tried to rub the water out of his eyes. It was a young woman, probably close to his own age, and she was half smiling and half smirking in his direction. "I'm sorry," James said, "I didn't know anyone else was out here with me."

"That's okay," she replied, "I thought I would be alone, too."

That was when James noticed the rather pleasant shape floating just beneath the water and realized that, like him, she was swimming only in her birthday suit. He stammered a little bit as he said, "Well, I guess we can both enjoy this hot springs, it's plenty big."

"Yes, it's a really nice pool. I love it here."

"If you don't mind my asking, where did you come from?" James thought it was a polite inquiry.

"Where did I come from? My people have been right here in this desert for as long as time existed."

"Oh, I see. So you are a Paiute?"

"Yes, I am. And if you don't mind my asking, where are your people from? The Warm Springs tribe?"

James chuckled a little, and then paused a moment. "My tribe is from the island of Japan."

"Wow, okay, I guess I missed on that one." She seemed embarrassed. "I've never actually met someone from Japan before. I didn't know they would be so tall."

James quickly said, "I'm an American. I was born here in Oregon. My parents are from Japan. As far as my height, I'm just a freak of nature, I guess."

"You don't look freaky to me. What's your name?"

"James, James Uschida. And yours?"

"I'm Talulah."

"Just Talulah?"

"Yeah, just Talulah, at least for now. By the way, I didn't mean to be a smart aleck when I said we had been here forever. I've been living near Burns and I was driving down here today when my wreck of a truck broke down."

"Oh, yeah, I saw a truck on the road about half a mile back. So, what are you going to do?"

"I've got a sleeping bag with me. I can unroll it in the bed of the truck. I'm spending the night here and then hoping to find a ride out tomorrow."

"I see. Well, you've found a ride out if you want a lift from me."

"Oh, I see. Well, great. That sounds fine. I'll stay close to the pool here after taking my morning bath. Please don't leave without me."

"Doesn't it matter to you what direction I'm driving out?" James was feeling some normal masculine impulses while chatting with this attractive mermaid, and he was also fascinated by her attitude. He wanted to know more about her, but he was sincerely concerned about her welfare.

"I'm at loose ends right now, James, and I'm not sure if it matters which direction I head. As long as it's not back towards

Burns."

James smiled at her, "Okay, then we'll head south towards Klamath Falls."

She didn't reply but simply continued to float there on the surface of the pool, unconcerned about her appearance, and seemingly unconcerned about the future. For the first time in his life, James began thinking what it would be like to be in love.

*****

After his swim James carefully carefully scrambled out of the pool, toweled off, donned his pants and shirt, and traipsed back to his campsite. He didn't have much food for dinner but he didn't mind. He decided to save most of what he did have for to-morrow if it was needed. From the wood he had collected he was able to build a nice fire and then sit on a blanket right next to it enjoying the flames and the soft evening breeze. A little while after sunset Talulah quietly appeared at the outer circle of the firelight.

"Do you mind if I join you?" she asked.

"Sure, that's fine," was the immediate reply.

She walked over to a place without any sharp rocks, per-haps three to four feet from him, and sat down crosslegged on the ground, even closer to the fire than James, without saying anything more. The two of them stayed there, close together but without further conversation for at least half an hour. James was feeling together with her while quixotically wondering why they were too far apart to even touch each other. Then it began to slowly rain, uneven drops falling softly to the ground. Still, Talulah said nothing, and did not look in his direction.

Finally James spoke first, "Aren't you going to get wet sleeping outside tonight?"

"I've done it before."

"Well, Talulah, you're welcome to share my tent tonight. It will sleep two people." He looked straight at her, lowering his head in order to catch her eyes, "You don't have anything to be worried about with me. I will be a complete gentleman. I'm not going to make any advances."

Looking back at him she replied, "I know that. Only a gentleman would use the term advances. And yes, it would be nice to get out of the rain."

They went over to the tent and after she decided there was room for two she retrieved her bag from the truck, along what looked like a pillow stuffed with rags. They both fell asleep to the sound of nearby bushes gently swaying in the breeze and the far off cooing of a ring necked dove. For James it was a deep and contented sleep. That's why, in the morning, he was surprised to find when he awoke her head resting on one of his shoulders. His arm was partly underneath her shoulder, and he was afraid that any movement would wake her. So he simply laid there, wide awake but not moving. He thought about his earlier feeling that this trip might provide a lot of memories. He was positive now that he had been correct. He had no idea, anymore than Talulah did, exactly which direction his life was going, but that didn't mean it had no purpose. He knew he wanted to help people heal in some way from the wounds caused by five long years of world war. It didn't matter whether the hurt was physical, emotional, created by the enemy, or self-inflicted. He intended to contribute to a society where people like his parents, or himself, or pastor Charlie, or Talulah, or anybody else who had been dealt a raw deal, would feel at home.

# PART THREE

*Wedgwood Funeral Home*              *19 August 1950*
*401 North Goose Lake Rd*
*Lakeview, Oregon*

*To all friends and associates of Benjamin D. Carter*

*As announced in the Lakeview Gazette, and in Mr. Carter's published obituary, funeral services will be held in our main sanctuary room on August 27$^{th}$, 1950.*

*Mr. Carter was the publisher and editor of the Lakeview Gazette for over thirty years. Details of the many community charities he supported, and some of the countless good deeds he performed, are contained in his official obituary as well as the newspaper article we published upon his decease.*

*As a friend of the family you are cordially invited to attend this funeral service, greet the family, and witness his internment, if you so choose. Any flowers may be sent to the address above.*

*Sincerely,*

*Winton Henderson*
*Funeral Director*
*Wedgewood Funeral Home*

# BLY, AUGUST 1950

## ONE

The funeral service filled the church in Lakeview. While Mr. Carter had been too good a newspaperman not to have made some enemies during his long tenure, none of them wanted the rest of the community to know that they still held grudges. The altar was surrounded by flowers, most of them homegrown. Though the pews were filled, the only sounds were hushed whispering and the folding and unfolding of the paper programs. James was hoping that the minister in charge was not one of those long winded types. He had attended funerals before where he was certain that all of the speakers were convinced the deceased was listening in. If that was the case today, James felt like telling them that Ben Carter would have been editing their remarks so they fit in a short obit or column.

Talulah sat next to him, quiet as a gravedigger waiting to go to work. She didn't like the white mans way of mourning; to her God was represented outdoors, not inside a puny building. If there was one thing the many tribes of the Paiute nation had in common, it was living under an endless sky. As endless as creation, to her way of thinking.

Nevertheless, she had adapted during the last couple of years to living in a small apartment with James. There were many beautiful walks in Klamath Falls, most of them along lakes or rivers with trees and bushes that changed color with the seasons, shedding and adopting colors unlike any she was used to in the desert. They took trips eastward into the Great Basin almost every other weekend, since James knew that she was strongly tied to her sense of place there.

She also liked weekends visiting with his parents at their small farm. She had hit it off with his mother, Aoko, who was even more soft spoken than Talulah. During one of their visits she had asked Talulah if she had a nick name when she was growing up. That was a question James had never thought to ask, assuming that her quiet dignity somehow forbid nick names. She replied that her childhood name was Tuley, pronounced with a long u, because she had been named after the Tule reeds that were so important in tribal weaving. Unfortunately, she had continued to talk about the beauty of Tule Lake south of town before she brought herself up short.

James father had been wincing at the mention of Tule Lake since his confinement at the relocation center there was still resonated within him in many ways. He seemed diminished by the war time experience, a thoroughly changed man, at least in James opinion. While he was fine when talking about the farm, he had little interest in what was happening in the world at large. He had become the exact opposite of Mr. Carter, the man who was being honored today.

"Hello there, James."

He rotated his head quickly towards the aisle, wondering who would be greeting him. It was Mrs. Carter, who was being helped down the aisle by a teenager, probably one of her grandsons. "We need to get you seated, come on," the youngster said, tugging at her coat sleeve.

"Hold on, sonny, I want to say hello to Mr. Uschida," she rasped back at him in a voice gone hoarse with crying. "And hello to the lovely young lady next to you...." she was now digging for a relationship to be expressed.

"Hello to you Alice," James stammered out, "and this is Talulah, my uh, best friend."

"Oh, best friend is it? You were always so polite, James. You know Ben used to tell me about your life after you left our home. Especially the endless search for more war balloons. Has that been given up?"

"No, not completely. But I'm thinking about it, because most people around here know about them now."

Mrs. Carter's daughter had suddenly appeared at her side. "Come on, Mom. The service is about to start. You can chat with the guests later."

The trio started slowly towards the front as James relaxed a little. He hadn't been expecting to talk with Mrs. Carter until after the service, and then in a line of mourners, not here in the middle of the church with everyone listening in. He glanced at Talulah, who was looking the other way. Perhaps she was upset with his description of their relationship. On the other hand, she was the one who insisted on simply cohabiting right now. After she had explained her views to him no further discussions on the subject had been held.

Sonorous organ music was starting to fill the sanctuary now and all eyes swung to the front as the minister entered. Okay, here we go, thought James with a deep sigh.

*****

After the service, which was mercifully short, James and Talulah drove to the cemetery with some of the other attendees. Everyone was invited but it looked like about half of the crowd had slipped away between the church and the graveyard. James thought that once someone started an endeavor they should see it through to the end. For her part, Talulah had never seen a cemetery burial, and she was wondering if there were ceremonial aspects.

As it turned out, the ceremony was minimal. The minister offered a few sentences of the 'ashes to ashes, dust to dust' variety and then sprinkled a handful of dirt on top of the wooden casket. Since afterwards the diggers would be heaping shovelfuls of dirt on top of that handful, James strained to find the meaning in the gesture. After leaving Lakeview he had not been attending any church, partly because he was busy, but mostly because he was uncertain of his being welcomed. Hostility towards Asian-Americans had increased after the war as details of the conflict in the Pacific Islands had emerged from prisoner of war accounts and other sources. Just as the military officials in charge of the internment program had treated both Japanese-Americans and Korean-Americans as if they were the enemy, many civilians tended to group all Asians into the same category.

Immediately after this last ceremony ended, he saw several of the older people there start walking over to him and Talulah.

"Ain't you that kid that boarded with Ben and Alice a while back?" The questioner was a man in his seventies, dressed much like Ben would have been had he decided to attend his own wake in other than spiritual garb.

"Yes, I am. My name is James," he extended his hand to the man as he spoke.

"I see," was the reply as the guy hesitatingly shook hands with James.

"And is this your sister?" an accompanying woman about the same age as the man inquired.

"No," said Talulah. "I'm not his sister. I'm his best friend."

James smiled wryly at her statement, while glancing around the grounds to see what the other attendees were doing. He saw Alice Carter being hustled into a waiting car and thought that he now understood the questions directed his way. These folks had been deployed to distract him while Mrs. Carter was leaving. Her daughter probably wanted no more to do with him and his companion.

"Can I ask you one more question, as long as you don't think that I'm prying," said the old man, who hadn't moved. He seemed to be addressing James only.

"Okay, sure."

"Are you and your friend here from a local tribe?"

"Not really. I'm from the Burns area." Talulah interrupted, not caring who he was addressing; she was going to talk back.

There was an awkward moment after she replied, when no one spoke. Then James said "I'm from an even more distant tribe. My parents emigrated to this state from Japan."

If the first moment of silence had been awkward, this one was downright embarrassing. Finally the man started to mumble something but it was unintelligible. His wife, if that's who she was, grabbed his upper arm and yanked on his Sunday suit. "We need to go, Harvey. I've got to fix some food for the grieving family."

They both turned away, neither of them smiling nor saying good bye, just walking off.

"Nice to meet you," James tossed the words after them but they evaporated into the still air.

"Let's go, too." Talulah put her arm around his shoulder and squeezed. "We have met our obligation here."

## TWO

The plan was to stop on their drive from Lakeview to Klamath Falls in order to visit the newly installed memorial to the victims of the explosion near Bly. The cause of the fatalities had only recently become uncensored, and coverage of the official releases resurrected the event that had altered so many lives, including James. Talulah hadn't been able to understand his quixotic mission to find other unexploded ordinance, no matter how hard he tried to explain it to her. She had no objection to his stopping at the memorial, of course, but as they wound their way up towards the high mountain she tried again to pry an answer out of James.

"Listen, James, I want you to stop and see the memorial, I really do. But I still find myself wondering why that experience is so dominant for you. I know that you knew the minister and his wife and all that, but I think you have spent more time concerned with that event than with your parent's experience in the internment camp. Think about what they must have gone through."

When he turned his head towards her to answer, she noticed that his eyes were damp. "What I haven't told you Tuley, is that I was invited to go with them. The minister himself asked me just a day or two before they went."

"But you had other things to do, I bet."

"That's not the point! I should have gone. I needed to be there. I had already heard about the war balloons from Mr. Carter. I would have known not to get near them. I could have saved their lives, Tuley, I could have saved lives. Charlie would still be married. He and his wife would have had their child. It's my fault, the whole damn thing is my fault."

Tears were now sliding down James face and Talulah was worried that he would lose control of the car, "Pull over to the side, James, let's get out and try to ground ourselves."

He pulled onto the shoulder of the road and stopped the car. They both got out started walking, hand in hand, shoulders rubbing together, a few steps into the wild grassland bordering the road. There was a fresh breeze up this high that seemed to instill calmness into James. He took a deep sigh, and Talulah held onto his hand with both of hers.

"Do you think you can take stopping at the memorial?" she asked quietly. "Maybe you need to wait a while longer."

"No way," James relied immediately. "I can take it. I'm sorry I got emotional, but I want to stop and see the actual place where the accident happened. It will help me process the whole thing."

Talulah was glad that James had shown some deep emotions, and she felt really included for the first time in the three years they had been together. But she could tell that talking further about things right now was not going to happen.

"Okay, we're on the road again, I'll drive," she was trying to sound upbeat as they jumped back in the old car.

There was a small wooden sign on the highway pointing to the right and saying memorial site. It was a wide road as it traversed a lovely meadow filled with the gently swaying grass. Then there was a Y intersection and they took the north branch marked for reaching the incident site and the memorial plaque. This road had been recently graded, probably for the dedication ceremony, but it still wasn't in the best shape as they drove higher and deeper into the surrounding forest. Finally they saw a parking area next to the road indicating they had reached the memorial site. There was a trail leading from the parking about forty yards further to a big rock elevated on a slate foundation, with a brass plaque on it's front. The tall trees, most of them Ponderosas, the bright green undergrowth and the scattered blue and red wildflowers presented a scene filled with nature's beauty and simplicity. The whole place had a quietness and peacefulness to it that was remarkable after their noisy, dusty road trip. The first thing that James noticed when they got nearer the monument was a tall Ponderosa pine tree behind it that was scarred and discolored from the blast.

"Wow, would you look at that tree," he nodded at it as they approached. "It is black with soot or something the first few feet and then it has those deep red scars."

"Yes, but it's not only still upright, I think it is going to keep growing. Some of these Ponderosas' survive even the hottest wild fires. Their bark is so thick it protects them really well."

"I think that's what I must need," James looked over at her, "I need to grow skin as thick as that bark. Just give me some time."

Talulah couldn't tell if he was being serious or not, but she decided to drop the matter as they reached the viewing square where several other people were standing. They could see the signage commemorating the event and the people staring at it, but it wasn't readable to them from a distance.

They approached slowly, almost reverently, so as not to disturb the people intently reading the plaque. The closest town to this wilderness area was Bly, and they both realized that relatives of the victims would be among the most likely people to visit the memorial. Even though it was only five years after the war, the rest of the nation had moved on to other matters to an amazing, and to James somewhat alarming, extent. Japan and Germany now had constitutions written by the British and Americans, and they were moving on as democracies. The Soviet Union, an allied power during the war, was now being demonized to such an extent that the former Axis powers almost seemed like pals.

One of the visitors stepped back and turned sideways as he motioned James and Talulah to step ahead. "Thank you," murmured James to the gentleman.

He and Talulah read the sign in silence and then reread it since the other people had not moved. After describing the circumstances it listed the names of all five children and Mrs. Turnbull, too. After five minutes that felt more like twenty-five, the group began to melt away from the plaque and turn back towards the parking area. One of the women looked at Talulah and asked her, rather suddenly, "So, are you Indian?"

Talulah stopped and said "Yes, ma'am, I am Paiute."

The woman then turned and looked at James, "What about you? Are you Paiute, too?"

"Why are you asking?" James said, trying not to sound bothered, since he was both annoyed but also a little curious.

"Because I've heard that there are some Japanese people who have been to see this memorial, and I just don't think that's right."

"Why is that?"

"Because it's about what they done. They shouldn't be proud of that. They should be ashamed."

James didn't know what to say. Was she talking about Japanese-Americans? Where was she getting her information, from some local gossip?

While he stood there thinking about what to say, a man, perhaps her husband, stepped to her side, "Well" he asked, "What's the answer to her question?"

"We're both Paiutes," James said sharply, and then he turned and walked back to his car. When he got there he looked behind him and didn't see Talulah. He watched while the other people got in their vehicle and left, but he still didn't see her. Walking back towards the memorial he caught a glimpse of her, perhaps twenty feet away, feeling the bark on a Ponderosa pine.

As he stopped by her side she said very gently, "Maybe you do need bark this thick, James. You must feel very wounded to be willing to deny your heritage." Tears were in her eyes as lifted her face to his, "I can't imagine that, I just can't."

# PART FOUR

*Dear James and Talulah,*                          *2 Nov, 50*

*Thanksgiving is coming. I write because we would like to make sure you can come to our Thanksgiving day dinner here at our house. Your little sister says that she can make it home from Ashland University on the bus. She said even bad weather won't stop her. Your little brother also wants to see you two. Who knows where he will be next year at this time? That's not to mention Dad. You guys haven't talked in a good while. I'll have all the trimmings from our own garden, don't bring any store bought stuff with you, not necessary. Call me soon and let me know for sure.*

*Lots of love, both you, Aoko*

# KLAMATH FALLS, NOVEMBER 1950

## ONE

It was a windy, cold Thanksgiving morning. James and Talulah had set their alarm, which they hated to do on one of their few days off from work, but it was necessary if they were to get to his folks place early enough to keep them happy. They were both bundled up, with plenty of layers of warm clothes, because they knew that a walk around the small farm would be part of the program no matter what the weather. He strained to hear Talulah over the noise of the engine and the roaring defroster when she was speaking.

"Isn't this your brother's senior year at Klamath High?"

"Yes," he half shouted back. "He was nine when they entered

the camp back in 42. He's on track to graduate in June."

"Your sister was the salutatorian last year, wasn't she?"

"Yeah, but little brother doesn't have anywhere near the grades that she did."

"Why do think that is?"

"Don't know. I just talk to Mom on the phone. Maybe you should ask him that when we're eating dinner today."

"Very funny, James. I'm sure he would like to discuss grades with the whole family listening in. Why not ask him about girls while I'm at it."

James started laughing, "Let's save out voices for when we get there. We will do enough gabbing today to make us hoarse. I will, anyway. You might be out in the kitchen whispering to Mom like usual."

Talulah gave him wry, sideways smirk, and then slid down in the passenger seat and closed her eyes for a quick nap. Even though James had replaced the old car with a newer one in September, it wasn't as if the thing had a radio in it, like the really new ones.

*****

The house was warm and filled with welcome baking smells when they entered. James and Talulah were greeted by the whole family before they could get out of the entryway. His mother was animated and more happy than he could remember to have all three children together. His sister had arrived the night before from her college. His little brother was growing taller, though not enough to match James anytime soon, if ever. Only his dad seemed unmoved by the get together, not saying much, and unbelievable as it was, offering a handshake first to Talulah and then James, not a hug.

"How is your schooling going, my little man," James wise-cracked to his brother.

"It is going, and it will soon be gone; I can't wait to get out," was the immediate reply.

"And then what?" James countered. "You've got to do something. There isn't much excitement around the farm these days."

"I've got a couple of pals, good guys, and the three of us are heading for southern California after we graduate. They have lots of jobs down there. They need set workers in L.A. and guys who can wield a hammer building new homes for the movie stars, stuff like that."

Both of the parents in the room were slowly shaking their heads back and forth, so James decided to change the subject.

"Okay then, how about you, sis?"

"I'm doing alright, big brother. The college experience is far different from Klamath High, but I am liking most everything right now. The cafeteria food is much better, I will say that."

Aoko smiled and said, "Wait until we eat today, child, and then tell me whose food you like best. Why don't you all sit down in the living room and I'll bring in the tea. Plus I can get back to my stove after that."

As they entered the living room James could see that nothing at all had changed from what he recalled from childhood. The couch and two easy chairs were exactly where they has always been. He would bet a month's salary that the grooves made in the carpet from the furniture weren't a half inch off from where they were ten years ago. The fireplace hearth held a curved metal wood carrier filled with the pinyon limbs his dad liked to burn.

The cheap plastic radio on the mantel still had it's antenna extended almost to the ceiling, and there was no TV, no phone, and no magazines in the room. The end table near his dad's chair held a couple of old newspapers and one thick book, probably a classic Japanese novel.

Talulah was in the kitchen helping Aoko, and his dad sat down in his regular chair. James, his brother, and his sister sat on the couch with the oldest one closest to their father and the other two in order by age. These were the same places they usually had occupied when the family talked, or when they listened to radio programs. James was ten years older than his sister, named Aoko Se after her mom, and eleven years older than Abe, his brother, named after Abraham Lincoln. They had both entered the camp at Tule Lake with his parents and so it was nearly nine years since they had lived with James at the farm. That was one reason his father felt more protective of Abe then he had of James. Other unspoken reasons included that James hadn't finished four years of college, was living with an Indian woman, didn't have an interest in farming, and thus was considered less than a success in his father's eyes.

"Why don't you tell us about yourself, James?" his sister asked. "You quizzed Abe and I, now it's your turn."

"Well, as you probably know, accounting is not a tremendously exciting career for the most part. But I make decent money, my co-workers are a nice bunch, and the hours are very regular."

"Is there room for movement, you know, promotions?"

"Not much at this company. It's pretty small, and of course Klamath Falls doesn't have a surplus of companies to be audited or anything. The economy is booming in bigger cities in Oregon, though. Eugene for one, and of course Portland took off during the war with all the shipbuilding projects."

"So are you thinking of moving?"

James saw Talulah and his mom entering with a tray full of hot tea and quickly cut off his sister with a slicing hand movement. He either didn't want his mom to hear her question, or perhaps Talulah.

His mother served the tea while Talulah tactfully sat down on the hearth rather than taking Aoko's easy chair. When she had finished pouring, she sat in her chair and smiled at her husband, "Why don't you tell your son and his girlfriend about the new vegetables we raised this year?"

John Uschida harrumphed. "The boy doesn't care about crops, mother. He's not a farmer. I bet he and this gal don't even plant vegetables."

Talulah spoke up, "Well Mr. Uschida, we do have a small vegetable garden."

"Oh for gosh sakes just call him John, dear," Mrs. Uschida sounded ready to harrumph herself.

"Yeah, Dad, and this here gal should be called Talulah, or Tuley if you want to. What has got your goat today, anyway?" James was trying to ask politely.

"Listen son, unlike me you were never incarcerated by your own government. I was. It makes a man question his own future, and that of his family. They tried to force me to sign a damn loyalty oath. I left my place of birth, my homeland and spent days on a stinking boat to emigrate here. Isn't that enough?"

His dad paused for a minute, seeming to collect his thoughts, perhaps wondering if he should proceed. He decided to, "Do you kids remember when we told you your uncle died during his last year in the camps?"

They all slowly nodded. James' uncle was the oldest of his dad's siblings, much older than John himself. James had always assumed he just passed from a heart attack in his sleep or something.

His father continued, "He actually wasn't in the camp when he died. It was in late October. We had been ordered to do day work for the area farmers like usual. We were harvesting pumpkins. Pumpkins that could be used for Halloween, or for pumpkin pie for the Thanksgiving holiday. When bed check was done it turned out that your uncle wasn't there. We thought that somehow he had missed the bus back from the fields, maybe he was in the john or something. We asked the guards to go look for him. His wife begged them. It was too damn cold that year for them to head out in the dark. They refused to go look. The next morning when we arrived at the fields he was still there. He had frozen to death during the night."

The kids were silent but not James' mother. She appeared apoplectic. "Stop that, John! We don't need to talk about the camps today, of all days. This is a day set aside to be thankful, to be grateful for what we do have, not disappointed in what we lost. Your children are all here, I'm here, and your farm is still here."

Turning to the others she said, "Okay, no more questions about the past. Let's focus on the future. James, what do you see coming for yourself? Marriage, children, what?"

Both Talulah and James sat up straighter. 'Good old Mom, way to completely change the subject' they were thinking.

"Maybe the internment camps isn't such a bad subject, Mom," James gave her a big smile to show he was joking. "Plus, I don't know how to answer your question. I haven't thought that far ahead."

"Uh oh," said Abe, "That's what mom and dad don't like about my plans."

As everyone but James' dad started to chuckle Aoko Se stepped in to help her brother out, "Just tell them that you have a four year plan like I did. That will probably work, at least until they ask to see your grades."

Since her husband didn't want to talk about their farm, Aoko started in describing the growing season they just went through. Everyone listened attentively except for James, whose mind was still stuck on his father's comments. When John questioned what right the government had to ask him for a loyalty oath, James couldn't help but think back to August and his disloyalty to his own heritage at the memorial site.

Where precisely did his loyalty lay? Was he as American as anyone else, or was he a Japanese-American who just happened to dodge being locked up during the war? What sort of future did he have in a rural town so near to the most notorious camp, and so far from the diversity of a big city. Maybe his little brother's heading for L.A. was a darn smart maneuver.

## TWO

It was Christmas time when James decided that they really needed to talk. A decision had been building inside James since Thanksgiving, maybe even since he had landed the accountant's job in Klamath Falls. Yes, the job was okay, his parents were basically okay, and Talulah, well, he wasn't sure if she was or not. They hadn't talked that much, really talked face to face, since the scene at the bomb memorial outside of Bly. She knew something big was on his mind, but she was willing to wait until he was able to express himself. Patience was just one more of her strong suits.

They were in the small living room of their inexpensive apartment, listening to a radio playing holiday music in the background, while looking out the window at the sparkling skiff of snow on the ground.

James subtly cleared his throat, "There's something I've been meaning to talk to you about, Talulah."

She quickly said, "I still don't think that you should waste Christmas money on one of those television sets." James' boss had been the first person they knew to invest in the latest fad.

"No, that's a very different subject than the one I had in mind."

"Well, I've got something else to share with you, too. But okay, you go first. What is it, James?"

"Talulah, I want to move up to Portland."

"Portland?" She sat forward on the couch and turned to look directly at him. "Why do you want to move that far? Do you have a job offer up there?"

"No, no job offer, but I think that jobs are pretty easy to find up there."

"They sure aren't down here. Are you thinking they would possibly hold your job for you here while you check things out in Portland?"

"I don't think they would. But it doesn't matter. I have no intention of returning to this area."

Talulah stared hard at him now, and was silent for a good time. Finally, she spoke, "What is your motivation for moving all the way to Portland? Especially when your parents are growing older?"

"I've already talked this over on with my dad. I called him earlier today. Quite frankly, he isn't the same since he came back from the camp. He doesn't seem to really care what I do. And as for my motivation, it's pretty simple. There are no other people here who look like me. I would like to live where I'm not the only Asian-American. It's not like I have any friends down here. The guys who were at Klamath High with me look the other way when I pass them on the street. I left the school to move to Lakeview before they all graduated. Most importantly, I want to live in a bigger city where they have many different types of people. Plus they have more libraries and museums in Portland. I need a place where I can do research on the topics that interest me."

"You mean on your danged balloons. When are you going to let that go? The war ended five years ago."

"I know, I know. But there are other things I'd like to study, like maybe Japanese history. This place is just too small. We already discussed the fact that we are going to wait a while to get married and have a family. We decided that a couple of months ago."

"I think you decided that well before then."

They both fell silent. Outside, clouds had been drifting across the sky and one now passed in front of the sun. The snow lost it's sparkle, while shade darkened their landscape. They could hear the few remaining leaves on the tree in front clatter in the breeze.

Talulah shivered and her voice sounded cold when she slowly began again, "James, I don't know for sure, but I think that I will not be going to Portland with you. This is as far away from my land as I ever want to be. I would not survive and prosper in a big city with it's noise, it's hordes of people, and also with that constant rain up there. I am a desert animal through and through. But you already knew that would be my attitude, didn't you?"

James had tears in his eyes. "I hoped against hope that you would want to come with me, Talulah. You should never doubt that for an instant. But yeah, I do understand your ties to the desert landscape that your tribe has inhabited for generations. It brings you such joy each time we visit. I think that you would be forever unhappy if I forced you to chose me over your homeland. I don't want to do that to you. I couldn't live with anymore guilt than I already have."

He paused to try to pull himself together. Then he lifted his head, "What did you want to talk about?"

Talulah took a deep breath, "It doesn't matter. Another time will do."

James was almost inaudible as he struggled the next sentence out, "I will never forget how I found you in the middle of that endless forest of sage brush. After I heard your voice in the hot springs I thought I was seeing a mirage. I don't know what more to say except what I find myself saying all too often in my life; I am so deeply sorry."

"I understand, James. You feel you must do this. We can't predict the future. Some things are meant to happen only once."

# PART FIVE

*Yame,*             *Jan 10th, 1951*

*Fukuoka Prefecture,*

*Japan, USOA*

*Dear Mr. Uschida,*

*Hello Sir. My name is Mina Miourshi and I am an American citizen. I am living now in Yame in Japan. My parents and I returned to Japan before the war for me to finish my schooling. We were unable to return stateside during the war, and my parents both died in Tokyo in the firestorms at the end of the war.*

*I mention these things not because I seek sympathy, but because I want you to understand why I am writing. Your name was given to me by the Japanese association in Oregon as someone I could trust who may be able to sponsor me.*

*I am eligible to return to the USA at this time only if I have a sponsor. I need someone who would agree to provide me with an address (one room) and accept financial responsibility for a short time. They said you have a good job (accountant) and perhaps available room.*

*I assure you, sir, that I am polite, educated through our high school highest grade, and speak and write English. I hope so much that you can help me temporarily. I would be forever grateful. Thank you, sir.*

*Sincerely,*

*Mina Miourshi*

# PORTLAND, JULY 1951

## ONE

Portland was quite an adjustment for a small town boy like James, but he had been handling it well in his opinion. The job search was frustrating to him, but it lasted only a short while. It turned out that there were new businesses, especially in exports, that were starting to boom now that the country was entering the fifties. That meant accounting firms were needed to deal with taxes, tariffs, write-offs relating to shipping goods to the military occupied areas of Japan and Germany under the Marshall Plan, and many other new government programs. Ike may have been a president who had never been a politician before, but he had big political ideas. There was even defense department money flowing to highway construction, an interstate system it was going to be called, because what good were all the missiles the department had if they couldn't be moved around when necessary?

After finding a steady job he had signed a long term lease on a small home in a nice area of town. It was a long walk to downtown but there was a bus route through his neighborhood that met his needs perfectly. He had a better car already but it was still not up to the level of most of the guys at the firm. He was saving his money diligently for his first brand new set of wheels, as well as his long range plan of buying a home. Since he didn't qualify for one of the low interest GI loans that were available to vets, he knew that he had to be ready with a substantial down payment when interest rates started falling.

Right now he was busy readying up the living room and kitchen for his new visitors to see. During the work week his place did get a little untidy, at least according to his standards. That's why he was happy that it was a Saturday afternoon when they were scheduled to arrive. After establishing himself in Portland he had joined a small group of other Japanese-American professional workers who met occasionally to talk about business opportunities and that sort of thing. Some of the meetings could be deadly dull, but it was a way to both burnish his resume and get to know people who might be able to help his future career. As it turned out, he was now the one being asked to help someone else. The association had given his name to a young Japanese woman who needed a sponsor in order to qualify to emigrate to the States. He had agreed to the idea since he did have an extra bedroom, and he could think of no way he could reasonably refuse. The chairman of the group was meeting the woman at the airport and driving her over to James' house.

He was drying dishes in the kitchen when the doorbell startled him. They were earlier than he expected. He whipped his apron off, hung up the dish towel, and took a peek in the hall mirror at his teeth, before opening the door. His friend from the association let out a vigorous "Hi, James, how are you?"

"I'm just fine, thank you," James replied while looking at the petite woman also standing on his stoop. She was looking down towards her feet with an embarrassed air about her, while saying nothing.

"James, I want you to meet Mina, our guest from Japan. Mina, this is James, who is your sponsor in Oregon, as I'm sure you know."

The woman looked up but did not meet his gaze directly, and slowly extended her hand in his direction. When he grasped it he was struck by how small and cold her had was. As for grip, her tiny hand seemed to melt inside his, even though he was being careful not to squeeze very hard.

"Please come in and sit down, both of you," James tried to smile warmly.

"I am going to help Mina with her luggage, but then I really can't stay," the man said as he turned and started walking back to his car.

*****

After Mina had entered the living room and sat on the couch she waited expectantly for James. He thanked her ride for the luggage, placed it near the hallway, and sat on a chair facing the couch but across the room. She still had an oversize brown coat on, and was clutching her purse. She didn't appear comfortable or relaxed. This was going to be an awkward conversation, he was sure. This woman appeared shy almost to the point of non-communicative, plus he hadn't really thought out what to say to her. The truth was he hadn't actually wanted a roommate, either male or female.

"I am glad that you have arrived here in Oregon, Mina," He was trying to sound upbeat, but felt himself failing. "I have an extra room for you to use. It's just at the end of the hallway, to the left. My room is to the right, and straight ahead is the bathroom.

Do you understand?"

"Yes, I speak English."

"Oh, of course you do. I knew that. I'm sorry."

She raised her hand, as if asking permission to speak. James was momentarily flummoxed, not knowing what to say. "Yes, Mina?"

"Is there only one bathroom?"

"Yes, I'm sorry, but that's all I have. The door has a strong lock on it."

He felt like the conversation had gone from awkward to stupid. What had he gotten himself into?

Mina looked right at him for the first time and said, "You don't have to be sorry for anything, Mr. Uschida. I am very, very grateful for someplace to say here in Portland. I thank you very much."

James relaxed a little. "I'm happy to help you out Mina. I hope that you are comfortable in your temporary quarters. I think that I may be able to help with your lob search too, since I know about a few of the companies in town, what they do, and who they employ at what wages. I will be glad to assist you on one condition."

As he paused, she looked at him again, with perhaps a little trepidation this time.

"What is that, Mr. Uschida?"

"It's that you please call me James, not Mr. Uschida. At least here in my home. Okay?"

She nodded her head up and down, "Sure."

"And at least for now, it is your home, too, Mina."

She quietly nodded again. He stood up and grabbed both of her bags, to take them down the hallway. She rose quickly and took one of them out of his hand. "I can help too, James."

*****

The job search went quickly. Mina was hired as a part time file clerk and bookkeeper with a small local realtor, primarily because she was good with numbers. The work was part time but the longer she was there the more they decided to expand her hours. She really liked the fact she could walk to work, especially since driving in her new country looked challenging to her. She enjoyed taking different routes through the neighborhood to see how nearby homes looked and what people were planting in their flower beds. She exhibited no great desire to explore downtown Portland, perhaps wanting to get used to neighborhood life in the United Sates before venturing out to sample everything that a big city had on offer.

James found that having someone living in the house with him worked out nicely from several aspects. First of all, she could cook. Not only that, but she knew how to fix several Japanese specialties. He had grown tired of his own cooking and the new food was fun to eat. Second, she was a big help with cleaning around the house, especially the kitchen. She claimed to be glad that she had hot water to soak the dishes in rather than the cold water she had used in Japan after the war. On more than one occasion James did find her standing at the sink with her hands in the warm water and no dishes to wash. She would be gazing out the kitchen window at the wooded back yard and seemed to be almost dozing with a peaceful look on her face.

Since the job Mina had didn't pay a lot of money, and since

James was satisfied with the accommodation they had come to, he soon decided to let her stay as long as she needed to get on her feet. She was pleasant enough to look at, pleasant to talk to, and pleasant to have around. Not exciting in any regard, but pleasant. He thought there might be bumps in the road ahead for her, but he never imagined how quickly the first one would come.

TWO

Life had been hard for Mina in Japan during the war and perhaps harder still after it ended. James understood all of that that within a week after her plane landed in Portland. She wasn't just shy, like many young Japanese-American women he had met. She was unwilling to talk at all about her life after she had returned to Japan in 1939 to study, which of course was exactly the wrong time.

After four weeks or so he discovered one of the reasons for her reticence. During that first month boarding with him he treated her with the utmost carefulness and respect. He tried to help her with certain things, like her job search, but also tried very hard not to intrude into her personal life or patronize her in any way. She did ask him numerous questions about the lifestyle of Americans and seemed interested in his replies, while quietly observing life in Portland and undoubtedly making judgements, which weren't shared with him. But all that changed thirty days into their relationship. It was on a Sunday night when she asked him to sit down at the dining table and let her tell him something important.

With her eyes glued to the floor Mina hesitatingly began, "I need to tell you that I think I am around week seven pregnant."

James was absolutely floored. She was so petite and so quiet and so humble that somehow the idea of her fooling around sexually was beyond his ken. He was speechless for a long time. Finally he said, "Can I ask who the father is?"

Mina was now softly crying, "It doesn't matter. He is in Japan. He will never ever come to the States. He doesn't know that I have a baby and he wouldn't care. I will never see him again."

She was looking increasingly uncomfortable and her tears were increasing, too. James didn't know what to say or what to think. He tried to soften his voice as he asked one more question, "Are you sure about this, Mina?"

She nodded her head up and down quickly, "Women know, James. My older sisters were born at home in Japan. My mother and I talked about things before she was killed. I should have told you sooner but I did want to make sure. But also, I feel like I should not try to hide anything from you. You have been so helpful and so generous to me."

"Okay, Mina, thank you for telling me. You will be fine. We have good medical facilities in this city. Let's talk more about this situation at some other time. I have a lot to absorb right now."

She bobbed her head up and down again as he noisily slid his chair out from the table. There would be no Sunday night TV on his new set tonight. He was retreating to his room to think and perhaps, for the first time in years, to pray.

After leaving it that night the next couple of weeks went on in their normal manner, at least without considering how things were festering in Jame's mind. Mina had found her job only a week after she arrived, a clerical position in a real estate company. She seemed to really enjoy living in America, especially the grocery shopping that she and James did together once a week. The store was so big to her, with so many types of vegetables and fruits under one roof. She had a habit of touching almost every single thing in the store that James had quietly pointed out to her made other customers look at her uneasily. In part she attracted attention because she still looked Japanese, mostly due to the clothes she had brought with her and the types of makeup she used. She seemed to be particularly noticed by men who may have been veterans of the second world war. Their stares tended to be less than friendly, but since Mina rarely looked people in the eye she appeared not to notice.

About three weeks after their prior conversation Mina began to show. James didn't know for sure but he thought it was because when she was home she took off the smocks and half-jackets she wore to work. He hoped that folks at her office were not starting to gossip. In any event, they again found themselves at the table an hour or so before they normally retired to their rooms for the night.

He came right to the point. "Mina, we have got to do something about your situation."

Her eyes filled with liquid and she just shook her head back and forth, unable to stammer out any words or to meet his gaze. Finally, one word emerged, "What?"

He knew there were no good options. There was no way for her to get unpregnant, and her situation would outrage people even if she wasn't fresh off the plane from Japan. He reached over and took her hand. "Mina, I want us to go down to the city offices tomorrow and apply for a marriage license."

He would never forget the silence that followed, which felt like half an hour to him, or the beseeching look in her eyes when she held his hand up and gently kissed it. The she collapsed into crying and he was damned if he didn't, too. There was a jumble of emotions within him bigger than the ocean he loved to gaze at, but foremost among them was the feeling that circumstances had compelled him to take the step he just took, and he might never know whether it was the right one.

THREE

The sun was directly overhead on a warm summer afternoon. It was a year after their decision to marry had been made official, but they weren't having an anniversary celebration. There was a light breeze playing with the tip tops of the fir trees in the yard. James and Mina sat on lounge chairs on the newly mown lawn sipping glasses of cold lemonade. After a chilly springtime it felt like a kind hearted delivery man had brought a little slice of heaven for them to slowly consume.

James turned to his wife with a smile and a look of contentment on his face, "It's really nice that they both went to sleep at the same time."

"Yes, it is. Can you imagine having twins who were on a different schedule from each other? Life would be much harder."

He smiled again, "I was just mentally calculating how great our lives are, Mina. Think about it; number one, I just got a promotion over two of my colleagues who had more time in at Turner and Mansen. Second, I'm finally starting to paying off a mortgage instead of just renting this place. Next, we have the two cutest daughters in the state of Oregon. And I have a spouse delivered to me straight from the Sun God that was shining on Japan when you wrote me your letter."

"Is there some gin mixed in with your lemonade, James?"

He chuckled, "No, I have not spiked my drink. Or yours either, for that matter." He looked straight at Mina. It was unusual for her to make a joke about anything. But she appeared as contented as he felt, and lately she was beginning to reveal more of her personality. During her pregnancy she had slept in her bedroom and after the twins were born their cribs had been placed in her room, too. But about three months after their birth, in the middle of a cold night, she had quietly crept into his bedroom and crawled under the covers with him. They had naturally cuddled together for warmth that first night, but consummated their marriage the next night. The last few weeks had been a period of intimacy that seemed to provide a psychological boost to both of them. She felt full acceptance, and he felt that his move to a brand new life in the big city was complete, as he was now trying to express.

"I am looking forward to our new life, Mina, that's all I'm trying to say."

She tried to reach over to to put her hand on top of his but the chairs were too far apart and she ended up touching his bicep, "You and me both James," she was murmuring as she patted his arm.

He turned his eyes straight at hers and covered them so the intense sun didn't get bother them, "I'm going down to the library to do some more research, you know, about how the war ended and stuff. I hope you don't mind me leaving you with the kids."

"Of course not, dear. We'll be fine. Just like when you're at work."

"Well, I hope we can find some way to get help for you,

maybe a maid once or twice a week, or perhaps a sitter, or something."

"Don't worry about that. You do your job and I'll do mine. You just said how lucky we are. Don't mess with success."

"Wow, that's some American slang there honey. I'm not sure that it would be a popular saying in Japan."

"We are both natural born citizens James. We are as fully American as anyone else."

"In that case dear, where is the apology for the internment camps that we're owed? My dad wants to know."

Mina was silent for a while, finally adding, "I don't think you will find the answer to that in your research."

# PART SIX

To: *The Japanese Association*          *January 5<sup>th</sup>, 1959*

*Dear gentlemen,*

*I am suspending my membership for the coming year and wanted to let you know that you will not be receiving my dues payment as previously scheduled. As you know I have been an active member for some time including sponsoring qualified newcomers to our city and business community. I think that more effort should be put into clear and transparent communication with all members of the association by the board members. This has not always happened in the past. I look forward to changes in the future, and a possible resumption of membership at that time.*

*Sincerely,*

*James Uschida*

# PORTLAND, JUNE 1958

## ONE

It was bring your parents to school day for the first graders in their small neighborhood grade school. For many of the kids this meant their mother since dad worked at the shipyard or the rail-yard and time off was hard to come by. James, however, had arranged to get a couple of hours off in the morning if he worked through lunch. The classroom was filled with excited, noisy children, and desks much too small for an adult to even think of sitting in. The teacher didn't take time to introduce herself to the parents and was instead trying to get the student's attention. She was an older woman who he sensed might not be in love with her job for much longer, if at all. He leaned against the wall and tried to hear the teacher as she raised her voice.

"Okay class, listen up. It's time for our next guest parent. The twins have brought their father, Mr. Uschida, to class with them today. He works for an important accounting firm downtown. Let's all listen to him, please."

As James walked to the front of the room he was thinking great, I'm supposed to say something exciting about accounting to a bunch of six year olds. "Hello everyone," he smiled at all the little rascals in front of him, most of whom were playing with their fingers, staring out the window, or trying to touch the hair of their closest classmate. "I'm here for Ally and Tally."

Mina had deferred to James when deciding on names, so he had chosen Ally in honor of his mother, Aoko, and Tally, well, because he said it rhymed with Ally.

"I work in an office downtown where I do lots of math, adding and subtracting big numbers. That helps businesses know how they are doing, you know, if they are making money or not."

He glanced around once more at the disinterested kids and decided to go straight to question time. "Do you have any questions about me or my job?"

The teacher rapped on her desk with her knuckles and barked loudly, "Come on now class, does anyone have a question for Mr. Uschida?"

One brave little boy in the back row stuck his hand in the air.

"Okay, Jack, what's your question?" the teacher said.

Looking straight at James the boy said, "What are you?"

James looked at him, unsure what the child wanted to know. "Well Jack, I'm an accountant, as I was just telling you."

The boy shook his head, "No, I mean what kind of people are you? Are you American?"

James now understood and looking steadily at him said, "Of course. Ally, Tally, and myself, we are all Americans."

The kid was not deterred, "But you don't look like us."

As James was formulating a reply, the teacher jumped in, "Jack, there are many races in America; white, black, brown, red, and so on. And there are many immigrants; Irish, Polish, Chinese, etc."

James waited for her to say more, but that statement appeared to do the job for her. He was not satisfied, however. "I am a Japanese-American, Jack. My parents were born in Japan. But I was born here in Oregon, just like my daughters were. In Japanese society I am called a Nisei or second generation, and Tally and Ally are Sansei, for third."

"Alright, I think we need to hear from our next parent," the teacher jumped in, evidently having had enough either of Jack's questions or of James answer, he couldn't tell.

James glance at his two daughters, who both looked happy enough, and then quietly left the room and headed for work.

*****

That night at dinner both Ally and Tally were telling their Mom and James about the other parents, "There was a real dentist, you know, one who pulls teeth." They were both talking at the same time, "And a guy who said he was a policeman, a detective, even though he didn't have a uniform."

"I see, dears," Mina interrupted, "but what about your father? Was he a hit?"

The two girls looked at each other. "Yeah, he was good," Tally offered. "And he told them we were Japanese," added Ally.

"But you're not Japanese," said Mina. "You were born in the United States. That makes you an American." She seemed more forceful about this point than James had seen in the past.

"Okay, yeah, he said we were JapAmericans." Ally quickly said.

"Wait a minute, that's not the term I used," James jumped in, "I said Japanese-Americans."

Ally looked defensive and then her sister spoke up, "That's what the kids called us at recess, JapAmericans. It sounded more funny to them that way."

Mina stared at James, as if he needed to say more. He simply shrugged his shoulders, "Okay, look you two, let's talk some more after dinner about your day. Now I want you to eat while I hear from your mother about her day."

Mina was still looking his way and now started blinking her eyes. "Yes, James, I had an amazing day baking cookies and making your dinner and wondering what was going on at school."

"Oh, I see. Good. Let's eat."

TWO

After Mina had arrived New Years eve had fast become James' favorite night of the year. It was traditionally a big event in Japan of course, and over there it functioned as a holiday on it's own rather than as an ending to the "holiday season" as in the US. Balloons were a big feature of the event in Japan and this year James had searched throughout the Portland area to find colorful ones to give to his daughters, six to each of them to celebrate their age. In Portland on New Years Eve one had a better chance of seeing a few whites flakes than on Christmas, but raindrops were the norm and they were falling now. Mina had been baking all day and their home was filled with the warmth from the oven, the mouth watering smell of hot chocolate chip cookies, the giggling of a pair of happy children, and two very relaxed adults.

After their big dinner and dessert, they migrated to the living room. The Christmas tree was still up and it's lights were lit, plus the fireplace was crackling with the chunks of alder recently added. Ally and Tally were laying on the carpet figuring out puzzles they had been given as presents, while each twins' balloons were tied to separate chairs so they wouldn't get them mixed up.

James sat on the couch and put his arm around Mina's shoulder, smiling contentedly, "I really like to see the multi-colored balloons. I think that I would have been happy to live back in the 1800s when hot air ballooning was the rage. And some people still engage in ballooning today, with very colorful designs on them."

Mina nodded, "Yes, I understand that balloon festivals are being revived again in Japan, where it's always been a special kind of excitement. Maybe they have lots of schoolgirls working on constructing them, just like I did."

James slowly removed his arm from her shoulder and then squared himself to look directly at Mina. "Well now, you are going to have to tell me what you mean by that last comment, honey."

Mina was careful in her reply, "I thought you already knew what I meant. We talked when I first came to the US from Yame. As you know from your research, that's where balloons were built during the last months of the war. Balloons made of paper that were then filled with hydrogen and sent up in the hope they would drift over towards North America."

"Yeah, sure, the war balloons. But those were built in a military factory, I believe. You were too young to be a factory worker then. You were just starting in high school at that time, like maybe a freshman."

"James, you have to realize what the situation was like in Japan at that time. By the end of the war, all the young men, including high school aged boys, had been conscripted into either the military or the home guard. And there was no big factory. The government needed to use what was available. It decided there were plenty of trees, so it started taking alder bark skins that were delaminated, and using them to construct the yards and yards of ultra thin paper that it took to make just a single balloon. That meant they needed many young girls, girls with nimble fingers, to contribute dozens of hours of labor. All the girls in our public school were compelled to take part in this labor, as well as go to school. We didn't have any choice."

"Why haven't you mentioned anything about this to me in the past?"

"I don't like to dwell on the war years, you know that. Plus, you told me about your friend and his wife and what happened with that one balloon. I didn't want to make you feel bad." Tears had formed in Mina's eyes and she was beginning to slowly rock back and forth on the edge of the couch. "Does what happened in the past have to mean anything to us now?"

"What it means is that the balloon that killed those innocent children could have been manufactured with your help, Mina."

She swallowed hard, "We were children too, James, don't you understand that?" She had never spoken to him in such a sharp tone before, but he just continued to look at her with a mixture of doubt and sadness on his face, but without saying anything more.

She broke the quiet. "I ran into someone downtown that I need to tell you about."

"Let's not change the subject so quickly, Mina."

"But honey, I really think that you need to know this."

"I can't imagine who would be that important. Someone

from my office?"

"No, a former military guy. He said his name was Chase."

"What? Commander Chase! But how would he even know you? When did this happen?" Now James was on the edge of his seat.

"It happened when I was out shopping to get you a little something for New Years Eve . Something that I haven't had the time to give you yet." Mina got up off the couch and went back to their bedroom to retrieve the present.

As he waited James was pondering the turns in their conversation. Mina worked on war balloons? He was still dumbfounded. When she was placed in his house, did the Japanese association in Portland know this fact? If so, why not let him know?

And why had his reaction to the name Chase had been so excitable? He guessed he had thought of him as kind of a kindred soul ever since their meeting twelve long years ago. The idea that he was right here in the same city seemed amazing at first, but then why should it? Tillamook was only three hours away, and the base had been closed for nearly ten years. Chase would have gone somewhere, and Portland was the nearest big city. Not big enough evidently, to prevent some sort of chance encounter between Mina and the Commander.

She returned with a small square box with a ribbon wrapped around it. "Here," she said, with one of her small, enigmatic smiles.

He yanked the ribbon off and opened the box. Inside was a delicate round cup, with an accompanying saucer. He took out both pieces of pottery with interest. "And this is?" he said.

"It's a sake cup, and it will keep it hot, since now you like your sake warmed."

"Thank you," he replied, and then he dug a business card out of the cup. It read;

Chase Cunningham
Original Paintings, and other art objects
Displays at studio 19, Honor Street, Portland

"Wow, so he really has become an artist. That's what he said he wanted to do after the war. So again, how did you get this?"

"I was downtown looking around for holiday gifts and I saw this art gallery. The sake cup was displayed and so I walked in and started looking at it. Then a middle aged man, very distinguished looking, came up and asked if I needed help. It turned out that his name was Chase Cunningham and he was responsible for most of the paintings, but other people had made stuff, including the potter who did the sake cup. I found that out when he gave me his card after I had made my purchase. I remembered his name from when you told me about your quest for the war balloons. See, I do listen to you. He was excited to know that you were in Portland and he asked me to let you know that he'd love to get together with you sometime."

"Amazing." James replied, with his mind already drifting back to his trip twelve years ago to the Oregon coast. So much life had gone on since then. Leaving Klamath Falls and Talulah, relocating in the big city, marriage and the unexpected children. The war years seemed like another century. He knew that by now, if not earlier, the Soviet Union had completely replaced both Japan and Germany as the enemy in the publics mind. Why would anyone think that balloons with crude bombs had been sent aloft when intercontinental missile with nuclear warheads now existed? America had changed immensely, and there was an atmosphere that the country was on the cusp of even bigger changes.

"So are you going to contact him soon?" Mina asked quietly.

"Oh, sure, yes. I am going to get in touch with him very soon." James had come back to earth enough to realize how grateful he should be. "Thanks a lot for the gift, honey. Both the beautiful cup and the business card. It's a really nice way to start the new year."

Mina was so happy that they were off the subject of constructing war balloons she wasn't sure how to respond. "You're welcome James, and you have to know that I love you very much."

He moved back from the edge of the couch and hugged her with both arms. Then he slowly massaged his hands up and down her back drawing her even closer to him. With her face pressed against his upper chest he delicately kissed the top of her ear and whispered, "Believe me, I do know that dear."

## THREE

It was only two days into the new year when James and Chase met. They both wanted to renew their acquaintance as soon as possible. They were sitting at a small table in the art gallery Chase ran, which was closed for the evening. He had a coffee pot in his back office and had made them mugs of decaf along with providing some donuts he had secured form a local bakery that morning. He had the same erect posture and square jaw that James remembered but now he sported a neatly trimmed salt and pepper beard surrounding his face.

"It was really nice to meet your misses, James. She seemed

to be very personable and, if I may say so, proud of you and your status at work."

"Yes, Mina is great. And I expect she mentioned that we have twin daughters?"

"Yes she did. In the first grade. Sounds absolutely marvelous to an old bachelor like me. But as we try to catch up, I do have lots more questions for you. For starters, when you came to see me at Tillamook, had you already met Mina? Is she a Nisei like you?"

"Oh, well no. So much has happened since we first met, Commander. I actually ran into a different woman on my way back from Tillamook," James paused, realizing how silly his reply sounded.

"But that relationship didn't last. Then after I moved to Portland I sponsored Mina's application to come to the States from Japan in 1951. That was simply to help her out with her emigration, but after she arrived we hit it off and then decided to get married. We had twins right off the bat as it happened," he was rushing through the details, which Chase sensed.

"Wow, congratulations. Now please, never use the word commander again James. I am just Chase today. And you are right, an awful lot of things have occurred since the end of the war. How about I tell you some of the basics about me while you coffee up. For instance, after receiving your information back then, one of the first things that I did after you left was to make myself aware of the whole war balloon project. It wasn't easy because of the war censorship but I found out what I could. Of course there was so much other stuff going on in Japan and America as the war ended. And using the atomic bomb on them changed the conversation, as well as having many horrific consequences. Not just for the poor victims, with no treatment for radiation burns existing, but for our reputation. They could have made a million paper balloons and not done the damage that one A-bomb did."

"Let's not even go there, sir. On one hand I feel terrible for all the innocent civilians killed over there, but as a loyal American I don't feel I should spend my time questioning war strategy. I believe that President Truman was following the best military advice that he could. And of course, the civilians killed near Bly, Oregon, were innocents, too."

"You're right, James. There was plenty of suffering and misery to go around. The two of us are both so lucky that we didn't serve overseas in either Europe or the Pacific. I couldn't have asked for a better posting than to be flying dirigibles up and down the Oregon coast. And the Japanese-American Army battalion was full of guys just a couple of years older than you. Believe me they saw some of the true ugliness of war on their assignments in the European theater. Before we move off the subject though, there's another thing I should mention to you. I read up on that tragedy down in the forest near where you worked. I tried to find out about all the individuals involved. In fact, I've been down there to see the monument. It's a very sobering setting, and a wonderful tribute to the young victims."

"I see. It's great that you did that. And of course when I said don't go there, I didn't mean that we couldn't talk about our past with each other. Of course we can. In fact I would like nothing more than to keep in regular touch with you, Chase. I've been too busy to make many friends here in Portland. You have a wonderful gallery here; your post military career has really taken off. I just hope that I start making enough money soon to be able to buy one of your incredible paintings, maybe one of the ones that are hanging on the walls right now or a future masterpiece."

"Okay, now you're talking. Let me show you a couple that I'm most proud of. Then you can start saving up tomorrow."

Chuckling, James stood up and said, "lead the way."

# PART SEVEN

Dear Mina,                                    21 May, 1964

*I've left this note for you to open when you wake. Our short conversation last night didn't give me enough time to fully explain why I'm going on this trip by myself. Believe me, I had no intention of offending you in any way. As you know I met with Chase last week and we had a very long conversation about some recent events in south-east Asia. I can't relay everything he said in this letter, but his information has caused me to think anew about a couple of long gone events in my life. I think that I need to visit my mom, and and maybe other people down in the Klamath area, and talk to them on my own. I'm convinced it will help clear my head about this stuff. I think you would be bored on such a trip. Plus now that our kids are in middle school I don't want to disrupt their studies. I know I could have waited a few weeks and we might have all gone together but I simply couldn't wait. Give them a kiss for me when thy wake up before they head for the school bus.*

*Love, James*

# TULE LAKE, MAY 1964

## ONE

Springtime had arrived in full in the Portland area. The air in the late afternoon was holding on to the day's warmth, and the cherry trees in the neighborhood park were already starting to drop their blossoms. James was walking all the way to the meeting with Chase, more than halfway from his home to downtown. Their meetings had by now adopted a regular routine, occurring twice a month, almost always on a Tuesday evening. That was when both of them were able to get away for a couple of hours of gabbing and hoisting a beer or two. Sometimes they met at a wine bar instead of a tavern, or even ate a bite at one of the nicer restaurants. Mostly though, it was a cold malt beverage in one of the the softly padded booths at the Maltby Bar. It was quiet enough in the booth to talk, and the spot was located equidistant between their two residences.

Bird songs, chattering squirrels, and the sound of distant lawnmowers surrounded James on his walk. He was tired of sitting behind a desk punching numbers, so he was finding his stroll to be very refreshing. He knew that since they last met Chase had taken a road trip through the Oregon high country desert all the way down to Lakeview. He was very interested in the coming trip report since he hadn't been down that way for quite a while.

Mina loved the coast, especially the forested areas south of Canon Beach. He thought maybe the tress, stunted by the fierce winter winds, reminded her of northern Japan. He had seen picture of decades old bonsai gardens that to his eye seemed awfully close to what mother nature had wrought along the seacoast without any human assistance. His girls had a fondness for Seaside, the first town they hit on the beach, with it's ubiquitous knick-knack-shops and cotton candy.

Chase was waiting for him with a ready smile as James slid into the booth. "Did you walk all the way down here?"

"Yeah, it was nice to have a dry day with the daylight staying longer. We made it through the big dark and now we're getting our reward."

Chase chuckled at the use of the local term for the wintertime. "Yes, these long beautiful days that we use to convince ourselves that the weather's not really that bad this far north."

"I bet it was pretty dry on the other side of the mountains on your trip."

"Kinda, sorta. We actually had two or three days that got showery, with the highs there on the desert plateau only in the low sixties. But we were gone for nine days, so still we had some decent days."

We meant Chase and his girlfriend Anna. He was now in

a steady relationship with a woman he had met at his gallery. James had started to wonder if the old bachelor was considering a change in his solo lifestyle. There had been no mention by him of their moving in together, much less considering the holy sacrament of marriage, but they both seemed quite happy to be with each other whenever the two couples went out. James also wondered if either Anna or Mina might be slightly envious of the bond that he and Chase had formed. The friendship between them was a strong one, and the men made a priority of their meetings. He had asked Mina about it once, but she denied any such feeling.

"So what would you say was the highlight of your trip?"

"I'm glad you asked that, my friend, because I do have a story to tell you, kind of a long one."

"Shoot."

"It goes all the way back to the incident outside Bly that you told me about, you know, the minister, his wife, and the school kids."

"Yes, Chase, I remember that incident well. I could give you the date, the names and any other info you would ask."

"Well then, have you been following the career of the Reverend Charlie?"

"Not really, all I know is that he stayed on at the church in Bly, at least for a while."

"Okay, well here goes the story from then up till now. I heard all of the details from one of the church families who happened to be lunching at the picnic table at the memorial site when we were there. First of all, the Reverend has remarried. In fact he is married to the older sister of one of the victims of the bombing."

"Okay. I can see that. Perhaps since they both lost someone

in the incident they have something in common."

"Yes, I think that could be the case. And of course they have their church and the community in Bly in common. Now for part two; what the newly formed couple did next is more extraordinary. They have been working as missionaries and health care workers for the last ten years at a leprosy compound in South Vietnam."

"Wow, that is some news. That takes real dedication. I think it's pretty damn dangerous also. Imagine the risks of the disease, the violence of the guerrilla war. Holy mo."

"You are absolutely right. Which brings me to part three of the story. Last year in South Vietnam the good Reverend got a do-over."

"Stop right there for a second, Chase. What do you mean by a do-over for heavens sake?"

"I mean a second chance. It turns out that the Viet Kong raided the compound last year. They wanted to kidnap the medical support personnel, such as the Reverend Charlie and his spouse, to work on their wounded troops. Maybe they wanted them to treat other sick people behind enemy lines, I don't know. In any event they went in at night and captured Reverend Charlie along with his wife, and a few other people there including children."

"Crap. They probably weren't being guarded. I mean who would mess with a camp full of diseases? But how did our side even find out about this if they took off with their captives?"

"That's just it. The Reverend refused to be taken out of the camp quietly. He threatened all kinds of resistance and noise unless they let the women and children go. Not only did they end up leaving his wife behind, it turns out that she was pregnant at the time and has since delivered the baby."

James sat there immobile, while feeling his mind racing around the top of his skull like a speedboat. Chase watched as he raised his eyes to the ceiling, as if searching for meaning. Then he put both elbows on the table and held his chin in his hands. Chase reached his hand over the table and grabbed him by the upper arm to steady him, "Are you okay, James?" he asked.

"Yeah, I'm alright," was the soft spoken reply. Looking up, he added, "Now I know what you meant, Chase. The Reverend tried so hard to save his poor wife and his unborn child after the bombing in Bly. I know how palpable his grief was. I'll never forget when I saw him after the incident. He was completely shattered. But now it turns out, seventeen years after that awful tragedy, he has somehow managed to save his next wife and their unborn child. Yes the good lord did give him a chance at redemption, but what's more, he was able to seize on that moment and do absolutely the right thing."

"Yeah, that is exactly what I meant. Of course the rest of the story is quite sad. The fact is that he hasn't been heard from since the abduction."

James was slowly shaking his head signaling no. "I understand your feeling, Chase, but imagine being in his place. The tremendous burden of guilt that he undoubtedly carried around with him since the incident in Bly has to have lifted. He did whatever he could both times, but this time he was successful. He saved his wife and child, and maybe others it sounds like. How many of us get that kind of opportunity twice in one lifetime?"

Chase was staring intently at James now, "You seem to be very affected by this news, James. I hope that I was sharing it the right way. I just thought that you deserved to know the latest about your old friend."

"Of course, Chase. The problem sure isn't with the messenger, and it's also not with the message. It's kind of overwhelming, that's all."

Chase waited a minute or two and then softly said, "Perhaps I can ask, since we are old friends, whether there's some guilt about something in your past that you are still carrying around, James."

Again there was silence for a minute or two before James' reply. Then a rueful smile creased his lips as he began, "There might be one or two things Chase, now that you mention it. But I am going to save them for another day, after I have fully digested today's conversation. Okay?"

"Sure that's okay, old buddy. I think there is one more thing that I must share with you right now though, no matter how full your head is with my first news. In fact, I don't think one beer is enough for me tonight, let's order another mug."

"Okay, I'm thirsty, too."

After signaling the bartender that they needed another round, Chase gave James a tight grimace and said, "My reserve unit has been called up."

"What!" James was astonished. "I thought that your time in the reserves was up."

"Nope. I have nine months left. Plus, of course, The Defense Department has the right to extend my deployment if it begins before my time is up, which this one will."

"So does this mean that you're heading for Nam?"

"Probably, but I don't know for sure yet. As you know after the war the government split the War Department services apart. The Army Air Corp is now the Air Force. That's what my reserve unit is."

"But you haven't done any flying since they closed the blimp base, right?"

"Yeah," Chase said chuckling, "there hasn't been much call for a former blimp pilot."

"It doesn't seem right that you should be dragged off to war at your age, my friend."

"Well, The services are desperate right now. And I dodged combat eighteen years ago, and then I chose to take Uncle Sam's reserve pay since then. I don't have any say in the matter now, James. It's all beyond my pay grade. My problem is I don't even know what our purpose is in Vietnam. I've become so immersed in creating my artwork that I really don't know what made us enter the conflict over there and why. What do you think?"

"I think that we are butting in where we have no business. It really ticks me off to see some of the terms being used for Asian people, and the caricatures of the North Vietnamese remind me of our portrayal of the Japanese during the last war. When will all this senseless conflict end? They told us that once the United Nations had been created, we would be getting rid of all the wars."

James was getting too emotional to speak any more. His buddy Chase had become a lodestone for him, a rock in his life that gave him a sense of being grounded and knowing what direction he was heading. Now all of that seemed up in the air again.

"It's probably getting time for us to go, James. If I had a third beer I might start crying into it. And you do have a long walk home. Do you want a lift?"

"No thanks. I need some time to ponder all this before I get back to the wife and kids. Thanks again for the information and the conversation. Try to enjoy the rest of your evening, Chase.

And please keep me informed about what's happening."

## TWO

The dust cloud slowly settled back down to earth while James sat in his car and waited before exiting. His mom was standing under the roof overhang on the front patio, pretty much out of the way of most of the cloud. Still he wondered to himself, how much extra dusting had she done over the last forty years due to his dad's insistence that getting their driveway paved was an unnecessary luxury? She held her arms out wide even while he was in the car signaling her happiness to see her oldest son again, a pleasure that he didn't afford her nearly often enough.

"Hi, Mom," he whispered in her ear as he hugged her carefully, her thin frame seeming lighter and frailer with each visit.

"Hi?" she said. "How about I love you, you wonderful mother."

He chuckled along with her. "Of course I love you, and it's great to hear some sassiness, too. It takes me back to when I was little."

She let go of him and pointed into the house, "Let's go sit for a while out on the back porch and talk, okay?"

"Of course, Mom." James was prepared for this ritual. His mother loved to sit and talk to him while gazing down to her flower beds in the back yard. They could also see past those beds to the huge vegetable garden that had been a commercial activity when his dad was alive, but now functioned solely as a family reservoir of healthy and inexpensive food. He wandered out to the back while she shuffled into the kitchen to pour lemonade and put cookies on a plate for them.

It had been three years since his dad passed, and the ugly truth was James didn't miss him that much, primarily because he had become so saddened and bitter towards the end that his company was not easy to bear. Since being released from the internment camps fifteen years before he had participated in groups seeking justice and compensation from the federal government for their unlawful imprisonment, but to no avail thus far. His mother, on the other hand, had two children still to raise, gardens to grow, meals to cook and many other activities to occupy her time. She was simply too busy to look back on the past. During their conversations she tried to get James to do the same thing, but it was almost as hard a sell with him as it was with her husband.

He sat down in the old, ratty patio chair that he favored and she put the cookies and lemonade next to him on a small rattan end table. As she slowly poured the drinks he said, "Mom, you don't have to serve me. I can pour my own lemonade."

"Does Mina actually allow you to do that?"

He glanced at her and saw that she was joking. "Boy, you are in a good mood today. Is it just my visit, or is something else going on?"

"Your little sister is getting married in two months."

"Really? Well I'll be danged. I thought there was still a dramatic shortage of available young Japanese men in these parts."

"That is still the case. She is marrying a Gaijin."

"My goodness. That is news. I'm not sure how happy pops would have been."

"Oh James. Time moves on. People don't care what happened during the war anymore."

"I sure hope that you're right. I want to believe that. But I think perhaps age is the determining factor. Many people who served in the war aren't as forgiving of people of other races as you think. People under forty, on the other hand, are not concerned. I think that another ten years or so will change many attitudes in this country."

"You mean the new rock music and the way women dress, things like that."

"No, Mom. It's much more than that. It's a change in values. If I could ever get you to come visit us in Portland, you would see lots of stuff that you haven't seen before. Attitudes are really loosening up on almost everything. There are women who get pregnant and either don't get married, or in some cases go to British Columbia to get the baby aborted."

She frowned for the first time since he had arrived. "Let's change the subject, James."

"If you don't want to look forward, then I have a question for you about the past."

"Oh gosh, way to trap your mom."

"No, it's important to me. It's one of the reasons that I came down here early this year, and without the kids."

"Okay, son, what is it?"

"I've been reading more articles about the camp at Tule Lake. One of the things that I've found out is that a few hundred of the internees renounced their American citizenship. Is that right?"

"Oh James, do we really need to go there again?"

"Please, Mom, just once more."

"Okay, some of the internees did renounce their American citizenship. It was an impossible choice that we were given, son.

109

The questionnaires were loaded. There was no good answer or right answer. It wasn't fair to begin with that our patriotism was challenged"

"But did you renounce Mom?"

"No, I did not."

"Did Dad renounce?"

His mother paused and lifted her eyes to meet his, "Yes, he did."

"Amazing, simply amazing, and to think that you never told me."

"There's a reason we never told you, my boy."

"What possible reason is that?"

"Your Dad got a second chance, that's what. He was also asked the renunciation question later on, so he was asked the question twice."

James was incredulous, "A do-over! Are you kidding me? I guess that's a fact that I should be growing used to by now."

"I don't know what you are talking about, but what I am saying is that your father was able to renounce his previous renunciation. That's why we were able to stay here instead of being shipped back to Japan. It happened after the camps were closed. They didn't know what to do with everyone, especially at Tule Lake. It had been the worst situation, with really bad management, and some untrustworthy guards. It's not that hard to understand son, the war was over and we considered this our home."

James was silent for a couple of minutes while slowly shaking his head, "I guess you're right, Mom. At least it's not hard for you to understand his reasoning and that's what counts. And while I intend to go see the camp for the first time after I leave you today, I agree that you and I don't need to go back to that history. I am not here to make life any harder for you."

She smiled the same sort of enigmatic smile he had seen on Mina's face, "You don't make life harder for me James, you make it more worthwhile. And I have a suggestion for you. There's a new visitor's center in town. They have maps that would make your drive to Tule Lake easier. I know it's not too far but those farming roads once you cross the California line can get confusing. I also think that there may not be anything left of the camp by now. I hear they sold all those cheap barracks to the ranchers to use for their farm animals."

"Okay, thanks Mom. I will check out everything you told me."

THREE

They did provide free maps at the visitor's center in Klamath Falls by the local Chamber of Commerce. Unfortunately, the only thing on the map was the small town of Tulelake and an actual body of water, spelled Tule Lake. There was no mention of the internment camp or any historical markers in that area. James was leaning on the tall wooden desk in the office studying the roads from Klamath Falls down to Tulelake and then up to Lakeview, when a tanned young man, who apparently worked in the office, approached him. He appeared to be only fourteen or fifteen years old, but tall for his age.

"Can I help you at all?" he said pleasantly.

James looked up. The young fellow was a clean looking, handsome teenager, with straight black hair worn longer than most guys up in Portland. At first James thought he might be trying for the "fringy" look that the papers said young men in both Portland and Seattle now favored. But his skin color wasn't tanned as James first thought, instead he could see at close range that it was light brown. Perhaps a little Asian ancestry, perhaps Indian, and maybe just a white guy who wasn't lily white; he couldn't tell.

"Yes, sure, I have a question for you," he replied. "I am looking for the internment camp that was used twenty years ago to house Japanese-Americans down near the town of Tulelake. I'm James by the way," he extended his right hand to the teenager.

"Hi," the kid had a firm grip as they shook, "I'm called JT. The question you asked has a fairly long answer, actually. Have you got a few minutes, or you in a hurry?"

"No hurry," James said.

"Okay, well there's a bench right outside where we can chat, and I can point out the street you need to take out of town," he was talking as he walked to the office door and motioned to James, who followed him out into the bright morning.

JT spread the map out on his lap after he sat down and pointed his finger towards the town of Tulelake. "You are going to go through the town first, and then as you drive southbound you will see a large fenced in area to your left. There's no sign or anything."

"What's inside the fence.?"

"Nothing much. The buildings have been sold off. There's the outline in the grass where most of them were. And there's tracks."

"Tracks?" James asked.

"You know, paths where people walked, tire tracks where the little Army Jeeps drove, that kind of stuff."

The tracks remark made James wonder again about an Indian background for the young man. "Are you from northern California or this area, if I may ask?"

"Oh, I'm from K Falls, born and raised," was the quick reply. He continued, "There is a stop that you might want to make before Tulelake, though."

"What's that?"

"There was another, smaller camp north of town. It was where the disloyal crowd was kept."

"Disloyal?"

"Well," JT was studying James as he spoke, "there were troublemakers in the main camp I guess, and some of the inhabitants had renounced their citizenship. They were kept in this area to the north of the main camp."

"Is there anything left of that camp?"

"There's one old building. And the fence is securely locked unlike at the main camp, so you won't be able to go in and walk around. But you will get to see what the buildings look like that housed the prisoners, uh, I mean the internees.

Plus, just a little ways down the road in a US Forest Service area headquarters. It's in charge of all the surrounding government land in the area. There's lava caves, lots of mountains, forested areas, all kinds of stuff once you cross the state line."

"I see."

"My mom works in that building, too. If you stop by, say high from me."

James started chuckling, "Okay, JT, I can do that. Just tell me her name and I'll say hello from you."

"It's Talulah."

When there was no reply for some time, JT started staring intently at James, who finally looked away from him as he asked,

"And where does your father work JT?"

"That's another long story, but I don't want to really get into that one."

The door from the office popped open and an older man started talking in a raised voice, "JT! We need you in here to help us move these files. Are you on a break or something?"

"No, I'm on my way back," he replied, quickly rising. Take it easy, mister, uh, Jim."

James watched as JT strolled over and re-entered the building, shutting the door quietly. Then he re-situated himself, turning his back fully away from the building towards the warming sun. That way no one in there could see as he began quietly tearing up.

FOUR

He was hopelessly lost not long after crossing the state line into California. Part of the issue, he now realized, was that he had inadvertently jumped onto State Line road instead of staying on the state highway. He wanted to see Talulah and the camp north of Tulelake first, and maybe get more guidance from her or one of the rangers at their building. The second issue was the hills and buttes and wild areas were so beautiful that he just kept ignoring road signs while he was eyeballing all of the scenery. The land that was not yet cultivated was filled with silvery green sagebrush and lingering spring wildflowers and big boulders of assorted sizes, shapes and colors. There were tiny signs pointing the way to lava tubes, or caves, which interested him too.

Finally he saw a dirt road that lead up to the crown of a hill so he hung a left and charged up to the summit. He had a three hundred and sixty degree view from the top. South of him was square mile upon square mile of country identical to what he had already driven through. To the north was a shimmering light blue lake he assumed must be Tule Lake. Eastward was a symmetrically shaped small butte with a top as flat as a pancake griddle. More importantly, to the northwest he saw a tall ridge and at it's base he could make out what he thought was a stone building with a parking lot.

Now that he had oriented himself, making it to the forest service office was no problem. He pulled into the dusty lot, filled at the far end with government trucks, checked his hair and his teeth in the car mirror, and slid out of the vehicle. There were flowering plants along the walkway into the one story building, indicating that some person inside might care about more than just paperwork.

A tall ranger in a carefully creased uniform sat behind a desk just inside the double doors.

"May I help you, sir?" he asked.

"I hope so, yes," James replied in his friendliest tone. "First of all though, I would like to inquire whether you have someone working here named Talulah."

"Yes sir, we do. Tuley is on her lunch period right now. If you notice out back of the office here, we have a trail that leads to the top of the ridge right behind us. Normally she walks up that trail to enjoy her sandwich in the fresh air with the view. You could wait inside for her to get back, or you can head up the trail yourself, if you like. I could probably tell you whatever you need to know, too, if it's about the surrounding area."

"Thanks. I think I feel like taking a walk. I've been in the car for a while." James nodded at the ranger and strode back out of the dim building into the sunshine. The trail looked like an honest one, gaining altitude right at the beginning and switchbacking up the hill. He thought briefly about how his accounting job did not lend itself to his staying in shape, but then took off up the hill.

He was more than halfway to the top before he spotted her. She was sitting on a flat rock perhaps ten feet off the trail and forty feet below the top of the ridge. She had on a wide brimmed ranger hat so he couldn't really make out her face, but the long jet black hair was a dead giveaway. He slowed his pace down so that he wouldn't be huffing and puffing too hard when he got to her.

He stopped on the trail below the rock and looked up at her, "Hello, Talulah, how are you?"

She lifted the brim of her hat to see him better. "My God, is it you, James?"

"Yes it is."

She stood up, "What are you doing out here?"

He shrugged his shoulders and stood there smiling for a minute or so, and said, "I would like to talk with you. Is that okay?"

"Of course it is," she sat back down as he scrambled up to the rock and placed himself next to her on it, but about three feet away.

"How did you find me?"

"Well, Talulah, I received directions down here from a young man working at the visitor center in Klamath Falls. A young man by the name of JT."

"Oh. Oh my goodness. He does work there part time. The school's history teacher recommended him. Did JT know who you were?"

"I don't think so. And just to be clear, I assume that what you mean is, did he know that he was talking to his father?'

Talulah took a deep breath, then removed her hat and turned her face upward into the sun, as if trying to bring in energy from that powerful source before she could reply to his question. Finally she turned back towards him,"Yes, James, you were talking to your son."

"Talulah, on earth how could you not let me know?"

" James", she slowly answered, "you chose to leave me, not the other way around. You chose to leave Klamath Falls and move all the way to Portland. You cut off contact after that point."

"But if I had any idea that you were pregnant maybe I would not have done that."

"Exactly. In other words perhaps you would have felt tied down. Tied down here, tied down to me, unable to do what your heart was telling you to do. I decided not to supply you with that rope. I have had no problems raising my son, and living my life after you left. I made the right decision, James. And JT will be turning sixteen next year so it's really too late to do things over any differently."

He sat still, internalizing what she had said. "Dang you Tuley, you always sound so wise, and so calm, and so deliberately thoughtful. How can I contest any words proceeding from such an oracle on high?"

She cracked open her first smile, "Then how about one more comment from your oracle; you are looking good, James. You look healthy and almost as young as I remember."

"Talk about me. You look identical to the woman I once knew. You haven't aged hardly at all. I always thought that you would be as beautiful at fifty as you were at 20."

She laughed, "Let's not get ahead of ourselves, I'm still a

ways away from fifty."

James sat there on the hard rock, uncertain about where to go in their conversation. At last he said, "How about this? I want to check out the camp down at Tule Lake where my parents were interned. I plan on camping hereabouts for a couple of days. Then maybe on Saturday on my way back I could stop in to see you and JT. I just want him to know what his father looks like. I won't cause any ruckus I promise. Then I'll head straight back to Portland. Is that alright?"

"That sounds fine."

"Okay. Thank you. By the way, what does JT stand for?"

"John Thomas. His first and middle initials."

"So, his granddads?"

"Yes. His granddad John on your side, and Thomas on my side."

James slowly rose from his seat on the rock, nodding his understanding of his son's name. "Thank you, Talulah. See you soon."

FIVE

A breeze was whispering though the tall pines as James sat at the wooden picnic table, full of emotion and ideas, some from many years in the past, and some from minutes ago. He was outside Bly at the war balloon memorial. He had wanted to revisit the shrine ever since Chase resurrected his past episode for him, along with the addendum about Pastor Charlie and the war in Vietnam.

His morning had been spent in Klamath Falls, talking with JT and Talulah. He didn't go into the visit he planned to this memorial since Tuley had already seen it and knew the Bly story of course. While he doubted if JT knew about the monument, he wanted to talk with him about other things. He wanted his son to think about the future; perhaps a visit to Portland, and maybe starting to plan right now to continue his education at a nearby college after he graduated high school.

Talulah's three room log home had the warmth and coziness of a small cabin with a dose of clever decorating tossed in. The small fireplace was made of rocks that Tuley had gathered herself from dry creeks in the outback. The loft upstairs had a skylight that focused one's view toward the tops of the surrounding trees. He could wee why JT loved it here and how it represented the kids' bond with the surrounding area's woods and mountains. When James left he had the feeling that he and his biological son were pleased to know each other, but probably unlikely to be in regular contact. JT liked rural Oregon and disliked big cities just as his mother did. James also surmised that his son was quite content with his life without a father he didn't know telling him what he should be doing with the rest of it.

For her part, Tuley had accepted his suggestion that she and her son pay a visit to his mom. He would write to his mom first, explaining the situation, because a surprise visit from a new grandchild might be more excitement than she could readily take in. The question of how his wife would take the JT news was another important consideration. While she still kept many of her feelings well hidden, she did let him know what she thought on matters that were important to her, most especially their family. One of the thoughts pinging around in his overworked brain was that she had once asked him if two girls would be enough children for him, hinting that perhaps he wanted a son. Well now.

A gust of wind sailed through the highest limbs of the surrounding pines, but it didn't reach all the way down to him. He again glanced sideways at the only other people at the site. It was a family of three at the neighboring picnic table, and they didn't look like locals judging by either their clothes or choice of shoes. The mother and father were around his age, with a daughter who was in her early teens, perhaps a little older than his girls. They were definitely ethnic Japanese he thought, but talking to each other in such quiet voices that he couldn't tell if they were speaking English or not. He decided to acknowledge their sideways glances by rising from his bench, taking a few steps in their direction, and stopping with a slight bow.

"Good afternoon. How are you?"

The father replied in what turned out to be broken English, "Hello to you, sir. We are doing fine perhaps. We come to visit your shrine. We are so sorry for your loss."

James felt stymied. What exactly did the man mean? He replied, "Thank you sir. It is really sad that innocent people died here. It is also sad that people died in Japan at the end of the last war."

The man eyed him carefully. "Yes, many people died on our Island. Terrible things happened in Tokyo, Nagasaki and Hiroshima. But war brings about great death and destruction." He paused as if giving James time to comment, and when he didn't, continued, "That many people died does not change that the people who died here were both innocent and very young. They were not soldiers in any eyes. They were women and children. My family is ashamed of our country's actions. We hope you accept our apology."

James was speechless. He hadn't anticipated this sort of

statement. He was trying to come to terms with the depth of the man's emotions. Then to his surprise the young woman spoke up, "I was born after the war, but I too feel guilt for what happened to these children. It was not right. War can't be used as an excuse. It was simply not right."

James smiled at her and then slightly bowed again to her parents, "I have daughters who are not much younger than yours. I would be very proud of them for such an expression of regret. And may I say her English is excellent. I would like someday to visit the birthplace of my parents in Japan. When I do I can only hope that my apologies are accepted as I accept yours today."

With that oddly stilted reply he left their table and headed back to his car. He was incredulous that anyone in Japan even knew of the bombing in Bly. He was also amazed at the expression of guilt, which was an emotion he tried carefully to camouflage rather than publicly express.

He thought back to the public portrayals of the enemy that he had witnessed less than twenty years ago. The explicit racism, included in letters to newspaper editors such as Ben Carter, against the "yellow horde". The treatment of American citizens of Japanese descent, such as his parents and younger siblings. The visceral reaction he had received at the local church door. Negative reactions to any expression of sympathy for the Japanese that had lasted for two decades.

He knew all the academic reasons for why the war against Japan happened from his research. Why and how it had joined the Axis powers; the oil embargo, the military leadership, etc. But how much did simple disdain for the other side, mixed with qualities such as racial arrogance, come into play? Especially in the debates about carpet bombings and the use of weapons of mass destruction? He had felt since high school like a pawn in a huge, nasty game, and he hated that feeling much more than he could possibly hate any other human being.

# PART EIGHT

TO: *Turner & Mansen*          *30 April, 1967*
    *Attn: Mr. Hancock*
    *Portland Offices*

*Dear Mr. Hancock,*

*I am enclosing with this note an undated letter of resignation from the firm which we both serve. As you know I have requested one extra week of leave time this year to be used in May. I believe that the declination of my request resulted from my admission to you that I intended to use that time to travel to San Francisco and join a protest against the war in Vietnam, an event scheduled in conjunction with New York and Washington D. C. marches.*

*While I understand that your personal political views may not coincide with mine, I think that single reason is insufficient to disallow a small amount of extra leave time. I have surely earned some consideration for my unstinting work and exemplary attendance record at our company. Furthermore, I feel that my Asian ancestry may be playing role in your decision. Since 1964 such discrimination on the basis of one's ethnic background has been illegal. I will be taking the requested time off, regardless of your decision. Should you choose to date and submit my letter as a result, I may well decide to take legal action based on your action.*

*This great country of ours, and it's citizens, suffered much during the war that ended in 1945 as well as in the Korean conflict. Indeed, civilians here in the state of Oregon were killed in World War II, just as draftees from this state are sacrificing their lives in Vietnam today. I strongly believe that all countries in Asia should be left to themselves if they are not presenting a clear and present danger to our country. To do otherwise is contrary to the Constitution and the vision that the founders of the Republic had for this nation.*

*Sincerely,*

*James Uschida*

# SAN FRANCISCO, MAY, 1967

# ONE

James sat expectantly on the couch, turning to watch his daughters enter the room. "Please sit down, both of you.," he said, trying to sound like he wasn't ordering them around at their age.

After eating dinner he had asked Ally and Tally if they could talk to him in the living room for a minute or two before they started on their homework. They had both grown taller than he thought they would, considering Mina's small stature and the size of the twins at birth. They were finishing their junior year in high school though, and could almost be called young women now. Naturally he didn't think of his daughters as old enough yet to be called women, and he didn't want any of their male classmates to think of them that way either. His protectiveness was copied by Mina who, for her part, had already objected to them thinking of college anywhere outside of the Portland area. She had carefully pointed out to them the three capable four year schools within a short city bus ride from their home.

As they sat down in the living room, each of the twins believed the talk would again be about college and it's local availability. Dad would never be the one to talk with them about any female issues, and neither one of them was dating a special guy at this time. Tally had delicately floated the idea of attending a church camp this summer and she was still hoping for a yes on that. Maybe that discussion was coming. Ally was taking a summer school course, and she didn't think her father knew about all of her reasons, including one of the boys who would be there, but she was afraid he might know more than she thought. He was a very observant parent.

Neither of them expected his opening line, "I am going on a short trip next week, and I want to tell you girls why." He looked at each of them for a moment and then continued, "I will be taking a bus ride down to San Francisco with a group of other people to join the protests there against our government's current path in Vietnam."

To say that Ally and Tally were surprised was understatement of a high order. Their Dad had never seemed like a political activist to either of them. Mina had entered the room while he was talking and she was taking the news in stride, so apparently she already knew of his plans.

"Well, Dad, can I ask any questions about this?" Tally was the first one to speak after his pronouncement. Both parents thought that she took more after James, while Ally acted more in the Mina mold.

"Yeah, sure Tally. Go ahead."

I guess I would like to know first of all, why this particular issue has activated you so much, and second, why right now?"

"Okay, let me answer those questions in reverse order. The why now is because there are very big simultaneous marches being held in San Francisco, New York, and Washington D. C. This is an opportunity to show the people in charge how deep and widespread the national opposition to this war really is."

"As far as why this issue, that is a more complicated question for me to answer. Obviously you both already know most of the facts about this conflict, so I'm not going to lecture you on any of that. It's just become a very personal issue for me in part because of our family history. As you well know by now Japanese-Americans were illegally held in detention camps during World War II. Being treated like a prisoner in his own country had a devastating effect on your grandfather. Quite frankly I can't help but see some of the same dehumanization of Asians in many people's attitudes towards the Vietnamese. Why can't they form whatever kind of government they want to? We did back in 1776. Overseas powers tried to stop us, but they failed. I think we are being set up for failure in Vietnam, and I fear that many American lives will be lost unnecessarily. The conflict is also exacerbating anti-Asian feelings like I said. The longer it goes on, the more those feelings will intensify. Let's just stop the fighting now."

Silence slowly rolled across the room after James finished. Neither the twins or Mina had ever heard him go on about any subject like this before. Mina knew he had been burying emotions within himself about his research topics, but she didn't understand the connection between them until this remarkable statement. She was looking at her daughters who weren't making any head motions, either nodding or shaking them, and whose faces weren't easy to read, either. Now I know why James calls me enigmatic was the ironic thought on her mind when Tally again spoke up first, "Great, Dad. I support your decision. I agree with your analysis."

Somewhat surprised by her complete support, James rotated to face Ally next. She asked, almost plaintively, "I guess I still don't know why you have to go to San Francisco. Couldn't that be dangerous? Do you really need to join a huge mob like that?"

James replied directly to her, "Thanks for speaking your mind, Ally. I appreciate your concern. And yes, there might be some risk involved. But I think it will be a peaceful protest, at least I hope so. During the past few years we have witnessed thousands of African-Americans standing up for their rights in this country. I believe that it's time for Asian-Americans to do so, too."

"I see. Alright then, Dad. Whatever you want."

*****

Portland State College was nestled into an area of downtown Portland that was known as the U, or university district. The northern edge of campus was only four or five blocks from the new art museum that James had visited before. He was standing with a gaggle of students waiting for the chartered bus coming from Seattle to pick up the Portland area war protestors. A steady drizzle was falling, leading to even the most vocal students retreating inside their rain parkas and alternatively shivering and sniffling while waiting for the Seattleites.

James, who was also sunk down in his parka, was startled when he felt someone's hand placed on his shoulder from behind. "What?" he said, shuffling around.

"Hello there, Mr. Uschida," It was Anna, Chase's new wife.

"Oh, high, Anna. And for goodness sake, I'm James to you, not Mr. Uschida. What are you doing here? Are you in line for the bus to San Francisco?"

"No, I'm not. I didn't even know you could catch a bus to San Fran here at Portland State. Are you sure about that, James?"

"Yeah, thanks, I'm sure. It's a bus some organization chartered to take people down to the anti-war demonstrations happening this weekend."

"Neat. I didn't know anything about it. Is it alright if I tell Chase where you're going?"

James paused for a split second, "I guess so. I haven't mentioned the trip to him because I wasn't sure what his feelings about this protest are, you know, his serving in the military and all."

Anna looked closely at him, "Come on James, you should know him well enough by know to understand that he is anything but authoritarian minded. He isn't happy with this drawn out conflict in Asia anymore than I am. In fact, he has a couple of new paintings that are set in the South-east Asia jungle. One of them is a huge oil painting that has dozens of shades of green being ripped open by orange and red flashes. He is showing what the agent orange bombing is doing to the environment. That painting, along with one other that he did after his deployment, is being installed in the Portland Art Museum. He actually painted them over there and air mailed them home to me. I was just up there talking to them about their placement. Afterwards I walked down here to catch a bus back to my job. Do you have time to dash up there to see them before your bus?"

Perfectly timed with Anna's question, the air brakes of a big old bus hissed into their ears. They watched as the thing lumbered to a stop in from of the students. In the narrow window above the driver where the destination of a bus was usually showing, they read 'Industrial Workers of the World'.

"Wow," Anna exclaimed, "I thought that was a 1930's organization."

"Really?" James looked like he didn't know much about it. "I don't think it matters as long as it gets me where I want to go. But, say, do give Chase my congrats. I wish I did have time to go look at his exhibit. And to chat with him about the recent work you described. Do you know when he will be getting back?"

"Yes, I certainly do. He will arrive stateside the day after tomorrow, and then they are going to process his separation papers. I think they finally realized he's too much of an antique for modern warfare."

"That's great news, Anna. Tell him that I'll call as soon as I get back."

With a farewell smile James joined the line of people boarding the bus. As one of the last on he wasn't hopeful abut getting a great seat. He had brought a good book and a couple of candy bars in his rucksack, but the old bus looked crowded and the seats weren't very big. He also thought it might take a while to get back up to speed.

## TWO

It had been a long bus ride from Portland to San Francisco. James was sitting on the grass in a park in the city close to where the march was supposed to begin. The protestors would then wind their way through the city to the big football stadium where the speeches would be given. It was already becoming evident that all of the marchers would not fit in any stadium, no matter how big it was. Radio stations were announcing a crowd of at least 250,000 people, although nobody really knew.

James was still thinking about how hungry he was. The bus had made one stop for food on the way down, at about eight o'clock the previous evening. He had already consumed the few snacks he had brought with him. All forty-five people on the bus, including their African-American driver, had filed uneventfully into the small town cafe until James was stopped by the owner. No Asians allowed in my private business was his proclamation. The others who were already inside had debated leaving but their hunger won out. James returned to the bus where he sat in silence until everyone returned. A couple of riders had smuggled some french fries out in their pockets, and those cold fries were his only food until the ride was over.

A skinny bespectacled teenager sat down on the grass next to him, "Hey, how is it going?"

"Oh, okay I guess," James replied.

"I'm Colin, from Seattle," the kid said while extending his hand.

"James, from Portland."

Colin pulled a damp brown paper bag from his little backpack and extracted a white, lumpy substance from it.

"I've got a lettuce, tomato, and mayo sandwich with me. Would you like half?" Colin offered.

"You bet I would," James would have accepted any food, regardless of description, at this point.

The two of them munched away on the white bread sandwich halves while the rays of the sun on their backs were getting warmer and the crowd was growing. Colin had on a green camouflage jacket with Marine Corps insignia on it. When he turned his back to look at the size of the crowd James noticed a large orange and green paisley peace symbol covering the back of the jacket. Since a good portion of the assembled people were returning Vietnam vets James wondered if he had underestimated Colin's age. He looked more like a skateboarder than a Marine but James knew that anything was possible in San Francisco in the sixties.

"I appreciate the sandwich, Colin, but I will say a little bit of bologna on the thing would have helped a lot."

"Yeah, tell me about it. I go to the UW in Seattle and there is a cafe on the Ave where the owner takes pity on the starving students. He sells them these lettuce and tomato sandwiches for forty-five cents each. I nabbed three of them before I got on the bus coming down here."

Before James could reply loudspeakers started to erupt at various points in the park so he and Colin got to their feet and tried to listen. The March was evidently moving out, although not in a very organized fashion. The two of them fell in with a mass of long haired, sandal clad young people and started trekking up the street. There was an older woman passing through the marchers putting a single flower in the hair of all the women and most of the men. James couldn't help noticing that she was a little stumped by older guys with mostly bald heads and some of the buzz cut veterans.

They went marching along at a regular pace until they didn't. The pauses grew frustrating because this far back in the group nobody knew why they were stopping or starting again. James also decided that his hiking hadn't prepared him for this much concrete. After about an hour and a half they came to yet another stop. There were buildings on both sides of the street but he had ceased to pay attention to any of them. Since he wasn't from the bay area he had no idea what they were for, apartments or shops or businesses, he supposed. They were multistory, mostly stucco buildings perhaps housing a bit of everything; offices, lofts, meeting spaces, whatever. Colin was now separated from him by about twenty marchers. It looked like he was chatting with a young woman who held more interest for him than his new friend from Portland did. When James turned to look right behind himself he saw two men holding up a banner almost half as wide as the street. It was black and white with Asian script printed on it. It took a minute or two and then it clicked; he was located under a type of Viet Kong flag.

He heard the slamming of big doors first, then he heard the yelling and next the screaming. Bursting out of the building to his right had come a phalanx of men dressed in what appeared to be nazi uniforms. He stood there transfixed as they invaded the protesters swinging their billy clubs and kicking people with their heavy metal-toed boots. Amazingly, he found himself trying to read the insignia on their uniforms, and when one of the louts got close enough he could see it read American Nazi Party. He watched as one of the biggest guys took a roundhouse swing at his new friend Colin, who ducked under the swing as the man's glasses skidded off his face. In the style of a slapstick movie Colin then jumped up and down on the glass frames as the guy fell to the ground trying to retrieve them. Perhaps the scene in front of him was why he never saw it coming; his head was clobbered from the side by a huge fist and then a body came through the air from the other side smashing him in the opposite direction from the first blow. He staggered towards the sidewalk and then collapsed into the curbing, a searing pain in his skull the last sensation he felt.

THREE

Mina was so tired of waiting. Ever since her flight had arrived she had spent almost all of her time patiently sitting and waiting. First for her bags to be delivered from the aircraft, then for a taxi, next to get a visitors pass from the hospital, and now the never-ending wait for a doctor to tell her what was happening. She understood that a small, quiet Asian woman wouldn't get much attention in a busy public hospital that had all kinds of emergencies to deal with. But she knew next to nothing about James and his condition. What exactly had happened to him? All the administrator said on the phone the night before was that her husband was in the emergency room after a riot has occurred, and that Mina needed to fly down to the bay area immediately if not sooner. She had called Chase without knowing that he had only ben home for two hours. She had asked for a ride to the airport and some help deciphering the new airplane procedures, like checking your luggage inside the terminal instead of on the tarmac. He and Anna had instantly volunteered to help. She was thankful that her girls were old enough to look after themselves for a couple of days. The modern jet aeroplane had taken off on time and taken less time to get her down here than she had spent waiting since she arrived.

A tired looking doctor walked into the waiting room and glanced around. His eyes fell on her and he came and sat down next to her. "Are you Mrs. Uschida?" he asked.

"Yes, sir," she said quietly.

"Let's take a short walk to my office. It's right down the hallway on this floor. It's a much more private space."

As she rose and followed him out of the room Mina was starting to tear up. This couldn't be good news if someplace with more privacy was needed to convey it to her. The doctor went through his open door and motioned her to a chair.

He gave her a very brief, cryptic smile before immediately delivering the verdict, "Mrs. Uschida, I'm afraid that I have very bad news for you. Before you arrived here your husband started convulsing and we decided, after sedating him, that emergency brain surgery was required. I am very sorry to inform you of this, but your husband did not survive the surgery. We did our absolute best for him."

Mina sat there like a statue, immobile. She was absorbing the doctor's words into every fibre of her being. She swallowed hard and then managed to say, "I understand. Thank you for your efforts, Doctor."

"Obviously you may need a while to think about further questions regarding what you desire for funeral arrangements, what you want us to do with your husband's body, and that sort of thing. I know that you live a long ways away so there are multiple issues. Please feel free to stay here in my office while you think things through."

After first arriving in the United States Mina would have

been reluctant to answer directly back to an such an important figure clad in his white smock of medical authority. But she had changed during the last fifteen years and knew what she wanted to say in reply, "Thank you, but I have spent time on the plane down here and my time waiting in the hospital thinking about what I would do in case the worst happened. My husband and I both agreed to be cremated after we passed on. I will sign the necessary paperwork for that to be done here and then to have the ashes shipped to me when it is completed."

"Alright, I will get that paperwork for you delivered to my office immediately. I guess I might say that considering that the cause of your husband's death was accidental, and that he was only forty-one years old, you seem more composed than many of the people I deal with in these kind of sudden situations. I appreciate that, while knowing full well how much pain you must be feeling on the inside."

"Well Doctor, to be frank, when my husband left on this trip I tried to prepare myself for almost anything. He had begun acting differently in the last few months, quite honestly. I won't go into all the details with you but he was caught up in the politics of the war in Vietnam, and had even submitted a resignation letter to his employer. In some strange way events at the end of the war against Japan had come back to haunt him. Perhaps those events had never left him in the first place."

"I see," the doctor was mumbling his reply because he wasn't sure that he really did see what the woman meant. Then he added, more clearly, "Dramatic events, especially violent ones, can have a strong effect on our psyches. We began to see much more evidence of that after both World War II and the Korean conflict. A lot more research needs to be done on that subject. We don't even have a term for it yet. Shell shock and some of the old terms are horribly inadequate. Obviously, it is not really subject to any surgical remedy, at least almost no one believes that anymore."

Mina nodded her head in agreement but said nothing, because she thought the man might be thinking her husband was a war veteran, part of the Japanese-American brigade or something. She was looking down at her feet and noticed the floor was getting a few drops of water on it. The doctor got up quietly and exited the room.

Mina continued to sit there immobile, her eyes pouring down tears, but her mind in a different place. She knew James was gone, but was he at peace?


## FOUR


JT was driving very cautiously on the curvy dirt road. He was gaining altitude up a steep side of the ridge and there were no guard rails to stop the vehicle if the soft road surface caused him to lose traction around one of the corners. He chanced a quick look at his passenger to see how she was dealing with the drive and the long views down. Mina caught his glance and quickly smiled back. JT reminded her of James in so many respects, but he also came across as different in significant ways. His strong physical appearance was mirrored in a personality that was more confident and assured than James. He was at home in this outback environment, and he was completely at home in his own skin. After getting to know him she couldn't imagine him working as an accountant, or living in a big city, like his father had.

After returning to Portland and breaking the news to her daughters, the first call she made was not to Chase, or even to James' mother. It was to Talulah. She wanted her to know about James death, but she also asked if she could try to explain it to JT. Both he and Talulah appreciated the kindness.

James had been unable to hide the pride in his voice when he first told Mina about his son. After hearing about him, Mina was a firm believer that JT was a wonderful addition to James life, both a son to go with his two daughters, and a biological heir to carry his family line forward. She hadn't actually met the young man until yesterday, when she got off the train from Portland to Klamath Falls, but now she was certain that her idea had been the right one. JT had immediately agreed with her plan about spreading James' ashes and the two of them embarked on their mission early this morning.

After gaining the ridge top they entered an area of trees with sparse undergrowth, so there was little to see on either side of the road except for the trunks. They were headed to a viewpoint on the Abert Rim, a spot where one could look out as far as the eye could see and not reach the limits of the high desert and it's endlessly flowing sea of sagebrush. It was a place James had described to Mina as the highlight of one of his visits to this place, a land that he and JT, and yes, Talulah, loved like no other. With the breeze that was blowing today his ashes would drift along the high, tilted escarpment below the viewpoint and mingle with the rocks, bushes, fox holes, dry lakes, wild flowers, rabbitbrush, petrified wood, cactus, bird nests and dried antelope dung below.

Her eyes were misting over by the time she and JT walked to the far edge of the viewpoint and looked over the wooden fence.

"Do you want to talk about things or say a prayer before we release the ashes?" JT asked her quietly.

"Maybe after we are done." She noticed that his face wasn't completely dry either.

"Okay. I'm going to sing while I distribute them, if that's alright."

"Wonderful, JT."

He began to chant very softly and slowly, almost to himself, as he held the vase over the edge of the fence. His rhythmic voice started to rise as the breeze increased, and his body began to rock back and forth, seeming to be in time with the rushing wind and it's ebbing and flowing through the sky. When he reached what Mina, with her symphonic knowledge, would call a minor crescendo, he turned the vase upside down and the ashes began streaming out and into the wind, dancing and turning their way down and across the  vast expanse until they vanished to their straining eyes.

"I know that they are still going," Mina said almost to herself.

"I know that too," JT whispered.

*****

They migrated over to one of the picnic tables on the bluff and both sat at the same time and looked at one another.

"Tell me about my father, Mina. If you don't mind, that is."

"I don't mind at all, JT. Just bear in mind that I'm not the most eloquent english speaker you will ever meet."

"I don't need eloquence, just information. I know so little

about him."

"Okay. I guess I will start with the important stuff, at least the most important to me. Just ask any questions you want as we go."

She took a deep breath of the fresh air and started, "You know by now that your dad was technically a Nisei, that is a second generation Japanese-American. But that is just a label, perhaps useful in some data gathering project, but not nearly enough to explain how he thought of himself, or his life, or his family."

"Yeah, I understand. My mom said he was conflicted about his place in the world, whatever that means."

"Yes, JT, I think that's right. He felt he was in limbo between two worlds actually. I'd say it this way; he didn't know, at least until recently, whether he was Japanese-American or full tilt boogie American."

"Huh?"

"Let me explain what I mean by relating it back to his experiences at the end of World War II. First of all, his dad never wanted him to visit the family in the camps, and so he never did. James himself was never interned. Living with a nice family in a small town meant that he managed to avoid some of the worst aspects of the discriminatory treatment that other Nisei received, at least as far as I know. He didn't share everything with me."

"Second, and perhaps more important, there was the bomb incident in Bly."

"How did that change things?"

"Well, he saw firsthand the suffering of ordinary Americans, non-combatants. They were people that he knew; Pastor Charlie was a man he admired, the kids were ones he had met. After that event he wanted, in some part of himself, to disown his parents country, to deny his ethnic heritage. He searched for more bombs so that he could become something of an American hero, someone who had prevented more senseless deaths or woundings."

"But he never found any."

"He never found any real answers either, JT. But he kept on searching, and that came to define him. You probably don't know this, but after he left you on his last trip, heading back to Portland, he stopped at the Bly memorial one more time."

"Okay. So?"

"There was a visiting Japanese family there, expressing their remorse at what happened up on that mountain in those beautiful woods. James came home and talked to me for hours about their sense of collective guilt versus his feeling of personal guilt. He wanted to know why they felt so anguished about what their government had done when they weren't in any position to influence events. Their daughter wasn't even born at the time. I couldn't answer his questions, JT. I think only a well trained psychologist could have dealt with them. I think that his constant seeking was wearing him out. He had developed this facet of seeing behind what others said, and being able to perceive small variations in attitudes that people possessed. He could get upset over very small things."

"So why was he so concerned about the Vietnam war? That doesn't involve Japan. I don't feel personal guilt about what we are doing. Those thing are decided by people I will never meet and never understand, either."

"It goes back to that seeing behind peoples' attitudes. He told me that he thought blind patriotism was worse than no patriotism at all. To me the bottom line is that he finally felt a sense of collective guilt because the world he had come to choose, the all-out American one, was betraying his trust and exhibiting the old anti-Asian impulses."

JT leaned back, swallowing hard and looking out at the far-away horizon, "I trust that he has found peace now."

"I think that he has, JT. I really believe that, too. And I know one thing that he definitely would have wanted me to do. I'm inviting you, and your mom too if she wants to come, up to Portland to visit us. You can see where James lived. You can meet his darlings, as he called the twins. And you can meet Chase, his best friend. Chase paints beautiful images of this high country desert. I think that you and Talulah would like them."

"Thank you, Mina. I will talk to mom and start checking the train schedules as soon as we get back."

Standing to leave, they both stopped as they heard a Raven, just landed at the other picnic table, begin powerfully voicing his pleasure with the wind and his newly acquired view. It's head raised skyward while letting a chorus of opinion flood out into the airstream. They looked at each other, and their faces held the same picture of surprise, and then comfort.

# APRIL 1985

# EPILOGUE

Mina breathed a big sigh. Then she closed her eyes and said a short prayer. She was done with her reading, done with her mug of tea, and done with reminiscing. She was ready now to have the talk with both of her daughters. They would be arriving shortly, after both accepting her invitation from last week. She was making some of their favorite deserts and had told them to come over tonight for sweet pastries, decaf coffee and to catch up with each other.

Ally was coming by herself. She was a hard working woman now, who had established a solid career in business, using her BA in economics and ability to read Japanese to land a position in the import-export sector of a large company. She had a current boyfriend but their relationship was far from serious. She seemed in no hurry to agree to a long term commitment with anyone, much less think about children.

Tally, on the other hand, was happily married and her spouse was coming with her today. There were no grandchildren for Mina yet, but she had been told there was the prospect of one or two, which pleased her immensely.

Explaining to her other friends, such as the ladies from the church bible study group, about the relationship between Tally and her husband JT, was not a lot of fun for Mina. She had friends who still didn't quite get it. Of course there was no blood relationship between the two, or a marriage license would never have been issued. But JT was the biological son of Tally's step-father James. Both James and Mina had chosen in the past not to reveal to any acquaintances that the twins were not James' biological children. Even Chase and his wife were not informed of this fact until after James had passed away. The couple had revealed the facts to their children after they graduated from high school, although Mina had still chosen to say next to nothing about their actual father. She insisted that she had lost all touch with him long ago and that he never knew that she had conceived prior to departing Japan.

Mina had been the one who had praised JT for his maturity and his love of nature before either of her girls had ever met him. When he finally did make his long awaited trip to Portland to visit Mina, Tally had been struck by his good looks; the dark, vivid eyes and his extra long mahogany hair. He had a sense of quiet dignity that he carried with him, something that none of the guys she had met in Portland possessed. She and her sister both booked a return trip later that year to meet his mom, Talulah, who hadn't come up to Portland. They also wanted to explore the area where their dad had grown up and Jt had offered to show it to them.

By their twenties JT and Tally were each visiting the other quite often, though the exact reasons weren't fully divulged to either Talulah or Mina until they were sure what they wanted to do. After she graduated Portland State and JT's graduation from Oregon Tech, they told everyone that they were engaged. They tied the knot in a small, family only ceremony, in the trees outside Talulah's cabin. They started married life living and working in Ashland, just an hour or so from Klamath Falls. Because of their disparate relationships with James, Mina knew that they would be the ones most interested in every detail she now was going to share with them. They each knew only part of James' story, in fact less than the half-story they probably thought they knew. She believed they would welcome the full story. It was the right time, for both daughters, and it needed to be done. She was thinking a chance like this came along only once in a mother's lifetime. Or perhaps, as her late husband had said, twice.

\* \* \*

# ABOUT THE AUTHOR

## Corlan Arthur Carlson

Corlan Carlson was born in Shoshone County in the Bitterroot Mountains in northern Idaho. He has a BA in History from the University of Washington and an MA in Political Science from Western Washington University. He lives on one of the many islands in Puget Sound where he drinks coffee, writes and ruminates.

# BOOKS BY THIS AUTHOR

**Devils Canyon**

Taylor Clemons Book One

**Moses Coulee**

Taylor Clemons Book Two

**Frenchman Coulee**

Taylor Clemons Book Three

**Northwest Noir**

Benny Rhodes Book One

Made in the USA
Monee, IL
29 October 2020